THE WAY-PAVER

ff

ANNE DEVLIN
The Way-Paver

faber and faber

LONDON · BOSTON

First published in 1986 by
Faber and Faber Limited
3 Queen Square London WC1N 3AU

Typeset by Goodfellow & Egan Ltd., Cambridge
Printed in Great Britain by
Mackays of Chatham, Kent.

The following stories have previously been
published as follows: 'Passages' in *Threshold* and
Woman's Journal; 'The House' in *Argo* and the *Ulster
Tatler*; 'First Bite' in *Bananas*; 'The Journey to
Somewhere Else' in the *Irish Press* and *Cosmopolitan*;
'Naming the Names' in *Good Housekeeping*; 'Five
Notes After a Visit' in *Literary Review* and in *The Female Line*,
published by the Northern Ireland Women's Rights Movement;
'Passages', 'Naming the Names' and 'The Journey to
Somewhere Else' all appeared in *Introduction 8*, published by
Faber and Faber Limited.

British Library Cataloguing in Publication Data
Devlin, Anne
The way-paver
I. Title
823'.914 [F] PR6054.E92/
ISBN 0-571-14597-3

for Connal

CONTENTS

PASSAGES

I have a strange story to tell. Even now it is not easy for me to remember how much I did actually hear or see, and how much I imagined. The journey between the shore of memory and the landfall of imagination is an unknown distance, because for each voyager it is a passage through a different domain. This story has a little to do with mapping that passage, but only a little: it is also a confession.

In the summer of '72 I was travelling in Ireland, calling on friends in Dublin, seeing relatives in the West, putting minor touches to my book on Dreams, looking for more folk-tales, and eavesdropping on people's dreams without drawing too much attention to the fact that it was my profession. I have been involved in analysis for several years. I'm not popular with colleagues because they see me as a kind of 'pop' analyst – a collector of stories. And in a way that is what I am. On this occasion, while I was staying in Dublin at Sandycove in a house belonging to some friends who had gone abroad for a few months, a girl came to see me.

She had heard I was in Dublin, indeed she knew that I was expected to give a public lecture at Trinity that evening on the subject of my book and so she came to see me because she had a dream to tell me. This is not so strange as it sounds. I had asked several of my colleagues at the university if any of the undergraduates they taught would be prepared to volunteer unusual or disturbing dreams which might help in my research. I was not interested in individual analysis, or the concept of 'cure' – I made that perfectly clear: I was interested merely in the content of dream stories as a source for fiction. My earlier publication had been on 'History and the Imagination: A study of Nordic, Greek and Celtic Mythology'. My next inevitable step was to turn my attention to dream territory. I had advertised and asked for people with particularly unusual, disturbing or prophetic dreams to come forward; I had promised privacy in that I did not wish to know the identity of the people concerned.

An old college friend of mine who was teaching history at Trinity rang me on the morning the girl came to see me. He explained that one of his students had a dream to tell which she did not wish to write down but which she thought might be of interest to me. I agreed to see her at his insistence. This was the girl who came. I was more aware of the dangers of exposing dreams than most others: dreams are very confessional; they offer a power relationship to the hearer in that they ask for absolution. They are a freeing device for the speaker, but the sin has to rest with someone: the priest absolves the sin but he also carries it with him; like the Christ figure he carries the cross that others may be free. This was not a role I cherished or viewed with any great pleasure. I was very wary of people who did invite others to unburden themselves – the result could only be masochism or sadism: the wilful acceptance of suffering or the inflicting of pain: there was no other way. I would either be hurt or hurt in my turn: being human I could not remain neutral. I met the girl with extreme reluctance, and wondered at her motives for wishing to confront me with her story.

Her appearance did nothing to allay my fears; in fact, it increased what I already felt would be a momentous and disturbing meeting. I remember her now as looking very child-like: she had the look of a small elf – which some men find appealing. She was tense and anxious, as though at some point she had taken the decision to hold back. I did not like her much. I find that sort of woman manipulative; full of little betrayals, because of the insecurity of her knowing that she did not rank among the women. Fear was written all over her face.

She looked as if she were on the run from something. And I knew, because I had seen such cases before, that she was haunted. During our opening small talk her utterances came out in jagged phrases, exclamations, sentences begun then abandoned, then taken up with a different subject: she made so many promising beginnings yet never knew quite how to complete them. But in relation to one thing she was utterly articulate: the story she told.

This, then, was how she began:
'When I was thirteen I was invited to spend the long summer vacation at the home of a friend who lived in Dublin. Sheelagh Burke was at school with me, we both attended the Dominican Convent in Portstewart. I was a day-girl; my father owned a newspaper shop in the Diamond in Portstewart. Sheelagh was a boarder; her parents lived in Dublin, where her father had something to do with property investment. I was never very clear. The thing about the upper middle classes even in Ireland is that the source of their income is never very precisely located; it is only a petty bourgeois mentality like mine which would seek to pin people to their incomes.'

The girl had a disconcerting habit of standing back and analysing her statements – placing them in a social context, thereby dismissing her own assumptions. Her tutor said she was a natural historian, if only she had the confidence to follow it through. I understood too that there had been some disturbance in her studies of a few years, but was not clear about the nature of this, and had not asked. These thoughts were going through my mind as she continued.

'My parents were delighted at the invitation: this was pre-cisely why they had wanted me to go to grammar school – to make friends like Sheelagh Burke. The Burke house at Sandy-cove was not far from here, and it was remarkable. It was at the far end of that long stretch of coast road which runs away from Trinity corner in the direction of the Dun Laoghaire ferry terminal, beyond the Martello Tower and still further. I remember arriving there so well. The house formed part of a

5

terrace set back from the main road. There was a small green in front and a gravel path or drive separated the green from the four double-fronted Georgian houses which stood there; the house belonging to the Burkes was the last of the four – that is, the one furthest from Dublin city. Like the other houses it was three storeys high and had a basement, with a separate entrance by the railings outside the front door. The basement was something new in the way of houses to me. In a seaside town like Portstewart there is only the unrelenting parade of low-lying bungalows in wide bare salt-stripped gardens, occasionally relieved by some modern two-storey houses, a row or two of Victorian terraces and of course the Convent itself, a castle of Gothic proportions perched on the cliff face. I had never been in a house with a basement before, and absolutely nothing of the neighbourhood I grew up in equalled the elegance of this fine wide-roomed house, with its brass handles and porticoes, wooden stairways and cornices. A further treat was still to come with that house – the waves of the Irish Sea broke upon the back wall. The garden literally ran away to the sea. From the music-room windows we had uninterrupted views of the sea and the day marked out for us by the comings and goings of the Holyhead ferry.

'I was given a room at the top of the house on the same floor as Sheelagh and Peggy – who lived in – and the view from my window was of Howth Head. I even remember the colour of the room: it was a strong bold rose colour and the walls were full of prints of flowers and birds. The curtains matched the cover on the bed. I recorded every detail of this house, committed it to memory like I did my Latin grammar. I never questioned that this too was part of my general education. After a time it became clear to me why I had been asked to spend the summer with Sheelagh; she was lonely, there wasn't anyone else around. Her parents were remarkable by their absence. Her father, whom we saw fleetingly, flew in and out of Dublin airport with such regularity it made my head spin. Places like Zurich, Munich and New York crept in the conversation by way of explaining these disappearances. I think I met her mother as she was passing through the music-room one day on her way to lunch. And even though she lived in the house and was not flying in and out of the country, we saw even less of her. I recall that she said something like: "Hello, you're Sheelagh's little friend? How nice of you to come." The only other inhabitants of the house appeared to be a brother who was a student at UCD, reading Medicine or some suitably middle-class professional subject. Peggy, whom I have already mentioned, was a sort of housekeeper-cum-nanny; her role was never very clearly defined. And as Peggy was slow on her feet and found the stairs too much from time to time, there was a young girl living in also to help. She lived in the basement and was called Moraig. I said that Sheelagh's brother was an inhabitant, that was not strictly true; he had a flat somewhere in the city, and only came home at weekends to eat Peggy's Sunday lunch.

'You can imagine from this that we spent a good deal of time on our own, Sheelagh and I. We played tennis, or went swimming off the rocks at the bottom of the garden; occasionally we took long bus rides into the city and ended up having tea and cakes at Bewleys. I had never had tea in a café before, and certainly not without an adult present. It seemed to me, because of the absence of adults in our lives that summer, that we had in fact grown up; the world was unmoved by our innocence. When we ordered tea in Bewleys it appeared. No one said, as they might have done in a tea shop at home, "What are you two children up to?" They took us seriously in Dublin. I felt I had entered a newly sophisticated world. In a few short weeks of being at that house, my confidence grew. I discovered that beds left unmade were magically made up. Clothes, even socks, could be hurled around the room with no fear of losing them; they would reappear fresh and clean a few days later. The best china and glass was used without restraint; and, even if broken, was always replaced or renewed without fuss. It put all my mother's restraints and fussy little ways in perspective: "If you don't pick that up you will lose it; if you don't tidy that away it won't last; we can't use the best china, we might break it." For the first time I felt I had an answer to her. What did it matter when life could be lived like this? I knew then that something was ruined for me. I have dwelt rather long on this beginning because I wanted to remember what it was like up to the point when everything changed, and not to try to suppress any of the details. Perhaps, though, I have romanticized it a little, but I don't think so. The important thing is this is how it impressed me.

'The music room, as it was called, was a long rectangle running from front to back of the house on the ground floor. It was a very grand room with a marble fireplace, two squashy sofas and a couple of battered armchairs; it had a sanded pine floor and a large indestructible and rather tatty rug – which Sheelagh had said was Indian. This was considered the children's room. It had been abandoned to the Burke children several years before; the smarter apartments and drawing room, which was out of bounds to us, were on the floor above. I never knew why it earned the name the music room, except perhaps it might have referred to the volume of noise emanating from it; because the only concession to a musical instrument that I could see was an upright piano which nobody appeared to play or know how to, standing against the same wall as the fireplace. On the opposite wall to the piano and the fireplace ran row upon row of silent books, and I believe there was a record player somewhere. But I can't quite remember where it was situated. Long small-paned windows filled the short walls at either end of the room so that the light ran right through. From the Sandycove road to the Irish Sea the view was uninterrupted.

'In the evenings when the wind coming off the sea rattled the windows, it was often quite noisy and indeed airy in the music room, even after the curtains were drawn. And it was on one such occasion while sitting in front of the fire with the wind fanning the flames, when Moraig had retreated to her basement, and Peggy was in bed with a cold, that we conceived of the idea of whiling away the evening by telling ghost stories. That is, I would. Sheelagh never told stories. In fact, she could never remember the important details, and she would often have to turn to me and say: "What comes next? I forget."

'I began with a favourite of both of us. I was not very original. I often told the same story twice, but usually with embellishments or twists. And Sheelagh was such a good listener and such an awful rememberer that every time she heard the story she said it sounded different. This encouraged me tremendously. I began with a story of Le Fanu's about the expected visitors who never arrive: at one point in the evening the family who are waiting for the visitors hear the sound of carriage wheels on the gravel, they all rush outside and find no one. What I had not allowed for when I was telling this favourite tale of ours, was the fact that right outside the music room was a gravel drive. And, at precisely the part in the story when I started to explain that at the time the family heard the wheels of the carriage on the gravel, the expected visitor had died, at precisely that moment a car drew up very slowly on the gravel drive outside the music-room window. Sheelagh took one leap off the carpet where we were sitting in front of the fire and fled out of the room, saying she didn't want to hear any more. I was left in the music room, still sitting in front of the fire, amazed at her alacrity. Normally, I would have been laughing myself sick at my ability to scare her, as I had often done in the past, but the trouble was this time I had scared myself. The massive coincidence necessary to tell an effective ghost story had just

occurred. At precisely the time I was explaining the significance of ghostly wheels on gravel as a portent of death – a car
drew up. In all my years of telling ghost stories at school, and
arranging for bells to ring or doors to open at crucial
moments, I had never stage-managed anything so effective
as that car drawing up when it did.

'I found myself sitting in the dark of the room with only
the light from the fire throwing grotesque shadows on to the
walls and the groans of the wind whistling around me as
company. I knew then that I could not bring myself to move
through the darkness towards the door or beyond into the
dark hall and then up three flights of stairs past all those
closed doorways and little landings to my bed. I was riveted.
So I stayed sitting still with my back to the fire, watching the
silent occupants of the darkness, until I calmed down. Once
or twice I imagined I saw the handle of the door turning, so I
tried to think of something pleasant. But when I looked away
to the window all the elements of stories I had told in broad
daylight on the beach, or in the gym or the second-form
common room, began to reassemble around me. And I
wished I hadn't such a fertile imagination. Then, just when I
managed to convince myself of my silliness and was beginning to work out how I could make another story out of the
incident, something happened which arrested me so completely that I thought my heart would stop. From behind me
in the fire I heard a little cry; not a groan, like the wind made,
of that I am absolutely clear. It began like a short gasp and
became a rising crescendo of 'hah' sounds; each one was
following the one before, and getting louder each time. I
experienced a moment of such pure terror that I felt my heart
would burst with the strain as I waited for the gasps to reach
their topmost note. Suddenly, just as the sounds had come to
a peak, I felt myself propelled from the room and ran screaming upstairs. I take no responsibility for that action; a voice
simply broke from my throat which corresponded to screams.

10

'In this state, I ran up three flights and straight into the arms of the warm, white-clad and still smelling of sleep Peggy. She had been under sedation all day because of her cold when the screams brought her to the bannisters. Sheelagh was standing behind her, clutching Peggy's night-gown and howling like a lost dog. Peggy was furious rather than consoling. She smacked both of us to make me stop screeching and Sheelagh to stop howling, and then asked us what we thought we were up to. "Bringing the house down like that" was how she put it. Characteristically Sheelagh blamed me for scaring her by telling the story; I blamed her for leaving me downstairs. Peggy resorted to her usual threats of "Right, Madam. You go straight back to Portstewart in the morning. Do you hear?" And for the first time in the six weeks I had been there I wished she had meant it. I had had enough of the freedom of the place; inside a small voice that I thought I had grown out of was saying: "Oh Mammy, I want to go home." Eventually, she got us both back to bed. Calmed, and much scolded, and therefore reassured, I went to sleep.

'I am always afraid to go to sleep. I have been ever since that time, and still have lingering doubts about it. It has something to do with going to sleep with one reality and waking up with another. It was like this on that particular morning. It was late when I woke; the morning boat to Holyhead leaving Dun Laoghaire was already filling the space in the horizon between the shore and Howth Head at the half-way point. I did not wake up myself as I normally do, but was wakened instead by the arrival of Peggy carrying breakfast. She told me to eat up and get dressed and come downstairs when I was ready. There were two men who wished to talk to me. Sheelagh, she explained, was already awake and I could see her after I spoke to the men. She busied herself picking up my clothes and laying things out while I ate breakfast. What surprised me was that she stayed

11

until I had finished and then supervised my washing. I had reached the stage where I was bashful about dressing and wished she would go. But she didn't. When I was ready we went downstairs. I was absolutely convinced now that something momentous had occurred, "How come Moraig didn't bring breakfast this morning?" I asked, as I reached the foot of the stairs with the tray. Looking back, I am amazed at the ease with which I had become accustomed to being waited upon. Peggy did not answer but said: "Come and meet the gentlemen who would like to talk to you." We went into the music room and I have to admit to experiencing a momentary shudder as we passed through the door.

'My suspicions were further confirmed at finding Sheelagh's father there, along with two men. The room looked different in the morning light; below, the boat was slipping past Howth and out to the open sea. On the other side of me I caught sight of a number of cars parked on the green verge; there were some people moving up and down the basement steps. One of the men in the room moved between me and this view from the window. He shook hands and called himself Mr Maguire. He then introduced the other stranger, his friend Mr O'Rourke. I can't recall much of what they looked like except that they were both tall and Mr Maguire was heavier than Mr O'Rourke. But I guessed they were policemen.

'"We want you to tell us now," said Maguire, "what it was that made you scream out last night."

'I couldn't believe it; I turned to Peggy in alarm. Had she called the police because I had screamed? Before I could reply, Sheelagh's father uttered the first words he had ever spoken to me.

'"Now don't worry, just tell Mr Maguire what happened. No one is going to hurt you."

'Peggy squeezed my arm, to encourage me I expect, but immediately I decided that was precisely what they would do – hurt me – and burst into loud sobs. When I stopped

12

crying, they persisted with the questions and so I explained how the ghost story had frightened us. I explained about the wheels on the gravel drive; how Sheelagh had fled from the room leaving me; how I sat on until I thought I heard sounds coming from the fire behind me.

'"Voices from the flame?" Mr O'Rourke said, looking meaningfully. "You heard a voice talking to you from out of the fire?"

'"Now that's enough Jack!" Maguire said.

'"Well not exactly a voice talking, more calling out," I explained. I am quite convinced that O'Rourke felt himself in the presence of a mystic who was in touch with speaking flames. But the other policeman wasn't so sure about the presence of the Holy Ghost in the proceedings, he kept bringing me back to what I actually did hear.

'"Can you repeat the sounds you thought you heard?" he asked.

'"I'm not sure," I said, "but I'll try."

'I began to call in the way I thought I had heard the voice call out the evening before. To make the sound I had to take short gasps, and eventually when I was quite breathless I stopped.

'"Why did you stop?" Maguire asked.

'"Because I didn't hear the rest," I explained.

'"Why?"

'"Because I was screaming so loudly at the time."

'And that was all. The interview was over and so was the holiday. Sheelagh and her father drove me to the station later and I did return to Portstewart on that day after all. I would have been glad enough about it except that I felt I was going home in some disgrace, and I was not exactly sure why. Sheelagh spoke very little to me, she seemed very downcast, and told me that she was being sent to an aunt in the West of Ireland for the rest of the summer. "I hate it there. I'll go mad with boredom," she said. The last time I saw her she was waving goodbye from the platform at Connelly Station. She did not return to school in September, and she did not write to me as promised. My parents never questioned my early return as I was sure they would. I gave up telling stories after that.'

'But what happened? I asked. I found myself growing impatient. 'And what has all this to do with dreams?'

'You're rushing me,' she said. 'And I have to unfold it slowly. They never told me and I didn't ask because somewhere deep down I already knew it was something profoundly disturbing. Then, one day, when seven years had passed, the truth surfaced to confront me, and this is what happened. I went to Queen's as a first-year history student in '68; the first year of the disturbances in the city. But I wasn't really interested in politics and knew very little about what was happening, except that there were mass meetings in the union, the McMordie Hall and in the streets. It was the beginning of the civil rights movement, when educated Catholics had awakened to political consciousness. Coming from Portstewart I never had any sense of discrimination that Catholics in the city seemed to feel. It never occurred to me that there were official and unofficial histories. Or that Protestants could go through school never having heard of Parnell or the Land League. I always thought that history was simply a matter of scholarship. In the seminars during my first year at university the students were fighting and hacking and forging out of the whole mass of historical detail a theory which made it right for them to march through the streets of Belfast to demand equal rights for Catholics. It was the most exciting year of my life; inevitably I fell in love.

'He was a counterpoint to everything my father, with his little shop and cautious peace-keeping ways, stood for. He was outspoken and clever and courageous; he didn't care who he offended, and he held back for nothing and no one. Until that time I had spent my whole life living on the edge

14

of the kind of respectability that people who run a corner shop find necessary in order to secure a trade and therefore their livelihood. I had heard my father humour the diverse opinions of so many of the customers that I grew to believe opinions were something one expressed but did not necessarily believe in, or indeed act upon. As we ran a newsagent's it became the venue for discussion of current events, particularly on a Sunday morning, when the locals would stroll in to collect the "sundies" and debate the week's news at leisure.

'"It's about time O'Neill got the finger out over this free-trade business. Why should Lemass do all the running?"

'"Ah, now, Mr O'Neill's a good man," I can hear my father interrupt. "He sends his girl to the convent. Did you know that?"

'"No, it's not the same O'Neill. You're thinking of the brother."

'"It's not a brother; he's the man's uncle."

'"That's just the trouble, the government's full of O'Neills; it's very confusing."

'My father always had a good word to say about everyone. If any politician was criticized he was quick to find some redeeming feature. With the result that I too became something of an apologist when it came to historical circumstances. That is, until I found myself walking en route from the university to the City Hall beside a provoking and thoroughly objectionable undergraduate: John Mulhern. I remember going home for the weekend following some of the first civil rights marches Belfast had witnessed, and finding my father fuming over the early dispatches of the Sunday papers.

'"Fools and trouble-makers, that's what they are! We have a fine, peaceful little country here. What do they have to go making trouble for?"

'I kept my involvement a secret and refused to be drawn into any of the discussions in the shop which ranged during

15

the eleven o'clock Mass. It was a feature of most Sunday mornings that the women went to Mass while the men stayed in the papershop. Then I heard my father say, "I can't afford a political viewpoint!" as someone tried to draw him out. "That is a political viewpoint – pure petty bourgeoisie self-interest" was my unexpected reply. It came straight out of the mouth of John Mulhern. I knew I should not have said it (a) because I couldn't justify it, and (b) because I had as good as betrayed my father by taking sides against him in the shop. There was a deafening silence, so much so that you could actually hear the waves crashing along the wall of the promenade some distance down the hill.

'"That's the stuff! You young ones with your education will tell them boys at Stormont where to get off!" said the man who had provoked the row in the first place. My father, whose anger was all in his face until that point, burst out, "If that's all the good a university education has done for you, I rue the day you ever went to that place."

'The conversation was over. I fled into the back of the shop and he followed me. "Your mother and I broke our backs scraping and saving to give you a chance. If this is how you repay us you can take yourself out of here back to your friends in Belfast with their clever remarks and smart ways; but don't ever come here again, shaming me in front of my friends."

'We never talked about anything important after that; I withdrew and so did they. I was thrown almost completely on to my friends in the city until I ceased to come home at all. My parents had ceased to expect me to. Occasionally I suppose they would read about this march or that and would guess I was there.

'This is peripheral, I know, but I am coming to the point. I said the truth about that summer all those years before reappeared at a particular moment. I have given you all this detail because I am a historian and a materialist and some-

16

where in all these factors an answer may emerge as to why at this particular period in my life the truth, or a perception, should become clear to me.

'It was the sixth of January when we returned to Belfast from Derry after the civil rights march which had taken four days to reach Derry had been attacked at Burntollet Bridge. I remember we, John and I, and two other students who lived in his house, were all feeling very fragile, very tired, and yet strangely elated. Something had been brought to the surface in the façade of political life – the cracks were throwing all sorts of horrors out into the sunlight. I had never slept with John before until that night.

'We had begun to make love and I was lying back in the dark looking at him. I closed my eyes and suddenly I found myself crying out in a way which was strangely familiar: I uttered or heard myself utter a series of small gasps until at the point when the note rose to its highest point I opened my eyes. Then I screamed and screamed and screamed. I imagined that John would strangle me and screamed out in terror. After that the room was full of lights and voices. As soon as the lights came on of course I was no longer afraid of him. The other students in the house thought I ought to have a sedative so a doctor was called. He tried to get me to take a sleeping pill, but I only wanted to rid myself of what I knew. "She was murdered. Moraig was murdered. He strangled her." I was rambling on incoherently, as it must have appeared to the onlookers, trying to piece together parts of the story of seven years before. I felt bombarded by signs and images and the meaning of events. They persisted in making me take the sleeping pill and so I gave in. Afterwards I resented having done so, because when I did reawaken I knew that I had passed from that state for ever, and would never arrive at a perception so intensely felt again. With the morning and the new awareness my parents came, and with them a chill. As though they had brought with them the

17

bleak wind which blows in off the Atlantic along the prom and leaves small deposits of sea-salt in the corners of their mouths. I felt the ice kisses on my damp cheek and tasted the bitterness of those salt-years. Before them lay the wreck of a daughter in whom they had invested everything.

'The last communication I had had with my parents prior to that day was a letter from my mother on the first day of January wishing me well for the New Year and informing me of the death of Sheelagh Burke. She had driven off a cliff at Westpoint – near her aunt's house in Galway – a few days before. There is a faint irony in that; her banishment was from Dublin to Westpoint seven years before. It was as though everything had come full circle; some strange mystery had unravelled – wound down. I seem to remember that the tone of my mother's letter was half-reproachful as though in Sheelagh's death was some responsibility of mine. I put the letter in my bag and took it with me on the march; but I lost it somewhere on the road to Derry. I explain this detail again because it may also have been a factor prompting the truth of that evening when Moraig was murdered to the surface of my mind. You see, I too had come to feel that the whole event was the result of some strange invocation of mine. I had called up, or dreamed up, the death just as surely as if I had murdered Moraig.'

'But you didn't dream it; you say it happened!' I said, reminding her.

'I haven't told you the rest of the story.'

'So far you haven't told me anything original: this is either Sleeping Beauty or Alice in Wonderland!' I said irritably. 'But please go on.'

'Haven't you realized that at precisely the moment in my story when I was explaining the significance of wheels on the gravel drive as a sign of death, the car carrying the murderer drew up? I created the event. What is more I later heard a woman making love up to the point of strangulation when I began screaming for her. It was no mystical experience: I heard her cries coming up through the chimney passage. Apparently her bed was right next to the boxed-in fireplace in the basement. When I sat with my back to the fireplace I heard everything. Seven years later when I made love for the first time I re-experienced the earlier memory and found the truth.'

'The truth?'

'Yes. When I was making love and I opened my eyes one split second before I screamed out, I saw something. The face I was looking at was not the face of my lover.'

'Whose face did you see?'

'I saw Sheelagh's brother. I saw John Burke's face.'

We regarded each other openly for the first time, in the way two human beings do when the mask has slipped – stripped away either by love or fear – and familiar traces of another remembering show through.

'At what point in the story did you recognize me?' she asked.

'Very early on; but I wanted to hear you out. At one point you almost had me believing you were someone else. I found myself thinking that I was listening to another coincidental story. You changed the names and the house location; that was imaginative. But you rather over-dramatized my sister's death. She did not drive off the cliff at Westpoint. She died of a heroin overdose in a basement flat in Islington. She had become a drop-out a few years before and we lost touch with her. So you see reality is more ignominious. Still, she would have liked your version better – it romanticized her. But then I seem to remember you have a panache for that. Why did you come here with this memory? I find it all very painful.'

'Why did I come?'

She had no sympathy for my pain; I had not stopped her but made her angry instead.

'You can ask me that? I have spent three years of my life in a hospital. Did you know?'

I shook my head.

'I can't sleep with the light out; I can't lie in the dark in case I see your face. For three years I took their drugs and their treatments but I kept my secret because I knew the one thing which would cure me was that one day I would be able to confront you with the truth.'

'The truth? What is the truth?'

'You killed Moraig.'

'Your hallucination of one face on to another isn't proof of a person being a murderer.'

'Not proof – truth!' she said emphatically. 'The imagination presents or dramatizes as well as intuiting a reality which is nearer the truth than any perception we arrive at through understanding, that is what I believe. And that is what I came here to find out. If I haven't awoken to reality after all this time, then I have awoken to madness. If I'm not through to truth then I'm through to madness. I believe you murdered Moraig because I saw your face.'

'Have you told anyone else?'

'No one – not until now,' she said. 'I need an admission from you – not a denial. I am either sane or mad.'

'It's metaphysics. Sanity or insanity,' I said.

'It's not metaphysics. It's the difference between truth and lies.'

'Let me give you a better explanation of what happened – one you can live with. The car drawing up was a coincidence; it may or may not have had something to do with the murderer's arrival. But two half-hysterical little girls managed to convince themselves that they heard it and so it must be like that. A servant girl, Moraig, was murdered by her lover; and you heard her cries as you said through the chimney passage. Now there is another factor which you haven't mentioned. One of those little girls had a massive crush on her friend's brother. She also knew that he was friendly with Moraig. She knew because she saw them exchanging glances. Isn't it possible that you saw his face when your lover – also called John – was making love to you for the first time because that was the face you wanted to see? You fused the murder of Moraig and the desire to see me into one single incident. And you went to great lengths to say how much you loved this other John – I found it a total diversion, an unconvincing obsession with that part of the story. Was it in case I guessed that you chose him for the resemblance between the names? John's name and mine are the same in reality and in the story. Why?'

'Because I wanted you to remember,' she said. 'I wanted to see your fear, as you have seen mine. Nothing you have said convinces me that you did not kill Moraig.'

'Don't persist with this,' I warned her. 'I've offered you a way out. You have a strong healthy young mind now – don't pursue this fantasy path any further.'

'That is exactly why I came to see you. To find a way back to a path I once knew. I don't want an explanation or a denial but I need an admission of your guilt before I can break out of this . . .' She paused as though she knew the word but could not use it; it came out eventually '. . . nightmare!'

At that point she began to cry.

I watched her very closely and realized for the first time that she was wrong; she did not need an admission; she was already free. In the telling of her story she had changed. She had lost the haunted look: she had confessed. After a while when she was quieter, I asked: 'What became of John Mulhern – your lover? You didn't say.'

'After that night it wasn't the same between us. He was afraid of me, and I think I was of him. I was taken home for a while to Portstewart and nursed by my mother. A short time after that I was admitted to a sanitorium, as I have already

21

told you. I came to Dublin only this year, to resume my studies. They thought I was better out of the North. He became something in the paramilitary, and is very well known. I heard that he married someone recently, but I don't recall the details.'

'He didn't wait for you to heal?'

'No. He didn't wait.'

It was that time of day when the Holyhead ferry has passed the tip of Howth on its journey out to open sea; the sun shone on the rocks at Sandycove, and a woman, young, but a woman none the less – faint lines around her mouth marked her out – standing by a window, traced its slow passage forth. There would be many more comings and goings to and from the shore, and many more passages to make as time went by; but at the moment, all her attention was with this one.

I looked away from the window; and found myself alone in the room.

THE HOUSE

It's my own fault that I ended up here. I have no one to blame but myself. I trusted her, you see. I don't mind any more, sometimes I even enjoy it; sitting by the window most of the day and they leave me alone now. I still get visitors: she always comes. She needs my approval even after all this time. In the beginning when she started to go I used to cry a little. Now I don't shed any tears at all. The pain is like a knot in my chest, it tightens the worse the noise becomes. And it usually happens after her visits. Sometimes the knot is so tight I think I am going to cry out. But I usually manage to control this urge. I don't talk at all now, I learned my lesson. It was opening up to her in the first place which did it. I should never have started to talk, let alone listen; and yet I so longed to have an intimacy with someone. I kept remembering '78 and wishing I could go back to a time before I met her, when she was just a nodding stranger on the road.

It began with a dream: the image was that of the interior of a house. It was the house I lived in as a child, fused with the house Paul and I shared when we married. In the dream I started at the top of the house – in the attic, where I had my darkroom – and began to run down all the flights of stairs to the bottom. As I approached them, the stairs became greatly exaggerated and seemed endless. I ran down each flight never expecting to do more than descend to a landing at a time; but to my surprise, I ran down flight after flight without stopping and right out through the front door and into the street. I left my job a year after that dream began to haunt me; that was how she entered our lives.

I worked as a teacher in the Art Department of a school in which Paul was Head of Mathematics. We had worked there together for several years. I am not sure whether the dream propelled me into this action or whether it was a symptom, but I had never been very happy at the school. Until I finally

25

found the courage to tell Paul that I wished to give up teaching Art to apprentice boys and concentrate on making it as a photographer instead. It meant that for the first time in our marriage I would be dependent on Paul in the only way a man hates a woman to be dependent – financially. I say this in retrospect, at the time he assured me that he would be glad to support me: so I gave up teaching.

She was my replacement. And this more than anything frightens me: I made way for her. It's very strange how every detail of her arrival, her appointment, her comings and goings, attached themselves like side glances to my consciousness. Everywhere I looked she was there, not in the centre of my pictures but somewhere in the far corner, tucked away and watching, like an incidental presence quietly moving across the lawn towards the house. On the day she was appointed to my old job at the school, Paul came home and said: 'The new Art teacher is smashing; they picked her because she was so like you. You'd love her. She's very sensitive.' I hate being driven into friendships, so I did not respond. The rest was inevitable: I was not going to be allowed to ignore my replacement. The next thing I heard about her from Paul was that she badly needed somewhere to live before the start of the new term. 'Could she possibly stay with us until she finds somewhere?' he asked. To which I responded with alarm because I fear such intrusions: 'She's a stranger. How can we share our house with an absolute stranger? We know nothing about her.' I have such fears about new people entering my life – and always have had; it has something to do with the fact that strangers bring with them wounds about which we cannot know because we have not witnessed the progress of the stranger through a community known to us. But most of all I have a heightened paranoia about outsiders, fostered by a Catholic childhood. 'Never talk to strangers!' were my mother's parting words as

I set off to school as a child. I think she may have impressed this on me too effectively, because at the same time I am not a confident enough person to live in a house with anyone I haven't known for a very long time. And I regarded Paul, who took up with people effortlessly and would tell his life history to the man at the bus stop or the woman at the launderette, as a fool to live so dangerously. He in turn dismissed me as aloof, ungenerous and neurotic. 'If you met her, you'd change your mind,' he said.

I stayed clear until Christmas, when I met her at the staff Christmas Party at the school. The trouble with giving up teaching was that I hadn't really left the school: my friends were still there. I was too isolated and too wrapped up in my work to make other friendships. It was the first time that I was able to observe what my withdrawal from the group had done: I was in the rather peculiar position of not being a member of staff any more; my place had been taken, my substitute was there, but so too was I. Alice, for that was her name, had naturally allied herself at school with Paul; and indeed, because he was missing the comradeship at work which we both shared once, he had naturally teamed up with her. It was clearly an easy, effortless friendship. (He never did make friends with men.) And she filled the gap at work which my departure left. Paul had always been a very adaptable person – on the surface. In fact he never adapts but rather makes the circumstances adapt to him. He hates disruption and never wastes time worrying about the effects of change. He would look around for something ideally similar and either make it the same as the past by the sheer force of his personality or blur the differences so that he didn't see them. I am, on the other hand, one of those people who believes that we pay for such naivety – for taking such easy exits. Instead of coming with me, of seeing how our relationship could adjust and would be changed by what I had chosen to do, he had not moved at all in my direction. He had stayed with Alice. This was how I perceived the situation that night before Christmas when I stepped into the festooned staffroom.

I had come on later because some photographs were still in the developer and I couldn't leave them. Paul, irritated at having to go on alone, had nevertheless gone ahead because he said that he had promised to be there earlier to set up the drink. When I arrived, the room was already full of the familiar faces of my teaching days; but something in the way they stood together, side by side, not talking, something in the arrangement of the group told me clearly: Paul had stayed with Alice.

She was small and colourless, in fact if I recall anything clearly about her in those early days, it was that she wore black and sometimes toneless things like white and beige. I was, on the other hand, fond of bright yellows and oranges. That evening the contrast between us was one of colour; in every other way we were the same. We both had dark hair and dark eyes and the slim figures of girls. In the way some men sense a woman's sexual waywardness almost as soon as she's begun, Alice sensed my insecurity the moment I arrived. 'Gosh!' she said. 'As well as everything else I've heard about you – you would have to be beautiful!' She laughed, biting her lip. I was foolish enough to believe that when a man or a woman tells you that you are beautiful it means they like you. If I have learned anything from that time, I have learned what a fallacy that is. Beauty does not excite pleasure; more often it inspires envy, resentment, anger, hate, but rarely pleasure. In my experience most human beings are too maimed to let beauty pass them by; few have the humanity to leave the wild flower on the hillside, to take their moment of pleasure and be gone with just looking. Lately, I have become fat and dull, I don't attract

28

their anger or hate or resentment anymore. And if I'm quiet even the nurses won't bother me. I like it better this way. 'Paul never stops talking about you,' Alice breathlessly assured me. 'And as for the kids, they say that no one understood them like you. You're a hard person to follow. I feel like Miss Mouse beside you.'

Plainness makes some women manipulative: Alice was one of these. She spun a web of flattery into which I tumbled without regard. She really is a sensitive woman, I thought, when she told me how insecure I made her feel. Before long we were competing for who was the most insecure. 'Never mind how I look,' I said. 'This is just bluff. Inside I'm scared stiff.' From that moment in the evening until I left with Paul, Alice and I could not be parted or interrupted by anyone. Paul was not sure whether to feel pleased or annoyed; he had been ignored all evening by both of us. 'Have you found anywhere to live yet?' I asked, as we were preparing to leave. 'Well, no, actually I haven't found anywhere suitable and I'm feeling pretty miserable about the whole business.' 'Why don't you come and stay with us until you find somewhere?' I said, as though I had just thought of it. 'Thank you,' Paul said, squeezing my hand as we left. 'You really are a generous person.'

I invited Alice to stay in order to prove to Paul that I was capable of forming friendships with women. He had often accused me of a defensiveness in relation to other women. I explained it had nothing to do with our relationship, I simply found men easier – they were less preying. My mother had warned me as a child that there were three things I ought to be afraid of and on my guard against in life: they were fire, water, and other women. Perhaps I had decided that the time had come to challenge my mother's wisdom; because I set out to make Alice my friend.

She moved in with us on the first of January, and I remember I never greeted a new year with more hope than that one. However, my dreams were to leave me no peace. If anything, they intensified, and sometimes were so noisy and the voices in my ears so strong that I woke up in a sweat and spent five minutes grappling for the light switch. After three nights of bad dreams, I woke up finally and said to Paul, 'There is evil all around me. I am being warned about something but I don't know what!' Being a hard-headed mathematician, Paul was, to say the least, unsympathetic to my fears. He had no time for what he described as my primitive instincts. He hated all forms of religion and mysticism. As a Methodist from a working-class background, Paul's idea of wickedness amounted to no more than overspending, living lavishly, and getting sick – all of these things got in the way of work. If he had any God which was personal to him, I would say it was work. He was an only son whose delicate mother killed herself through long hours of strenuous labour in a spinning mill in Belfast. And I have often felt that he grew up with the impression from then on that no other sacrifice short of that from a woman would be good enough for him. His mother set too high a standard for anyone else to follow. I wish I had had the courage to give him up when I realized that was all that would satisfy him. It was Paul's idea of what proper work consisted of that eventually drove us apart. I think that, every morning he left me at home, and dashed off to make his nine o'clock classes with Alice, he resented me for what he could not see as work.

When we first met I was an art student with a massive loom in the hall of my flat – the loom was imported from Donegal. It came in the back of my father's car like a box of firewood, and together we had assembled it. The loom romanticized me for Paul; he saw in me the weaver his mother had been. But I moved away from producing wall hangings and rugs and became more interested in photography, and this he could not grant the same seriousness, it was not physical work like weaving. And in a year when he could see less and less output, he resented me even more. In such an environment I could not work and the isolation I felt was incalculable. Most mornings when I did get up, I cried in the bath. And I believe I had a phase of lying in my room and staring at the ceiling. Eventually I stopped taking pictures. It was then I turned to Alice. It seems we both did.

In the beginning she and I had long soul-mate conversations: Paul never talked much about his feelings and I was glad to have someone round to console me in my down periods. Alice always supported me. But I noticed that, when she encouraged me in a course of action away from Paul, she was always on hand to step into my place. When I didn't want to go out to dinner with him, or I didn't want to go to any more school parties because I wanted a more independent existence, Paul, feeling rejected, simply shrugged his shoulders and went ahead, not alone but with Alice. I am not blaming her, the ideas were my own, but she seemed to undermine my position by stepping in so readily when I stood up to Paul. As long as there were women like Alice, men like Paul would never accept the validity of my position.

Instead of finding that what I had gained was independence, I found that I had entered a state of non-existence. I no longer went out with Paul, Alice did. My friends no longer missed me because Alice so effectively slipped into my place that I began to wonder why I still remained around at all. Then the dream came back and I began to understand a little more. In its reappearance the dream took a different form; I recognized it as the same dream, only a continuation. This time, after I left the house and rushed out into the street, I found myself alone on a dark road where I passed several houses, all of which were similar to the one I had just rushed out of. The problem which confronted me was what to do next? I had a growing sense of alarm because although I knew it was good to be free from the house I had previously inhabited, I realized I would have to make a decision to get indoors again to a place of safety before nightfall. Time was running out on me and I knew I would have to make up my mind soon. While I understood the nature of the dream in relation to my own struggle into independent life with Paul, the answer to the puzzle evaded me: if I am to escape, I thought, how am I to escape in such a way that I don't end up on the path leading to the same place as when I started out? I had given up teaching art and rebelled against the confines of my relationship with Paul precisely because I felt confined. But my break for freedom had actually resulted in a greater confinement: I had no place. Escape had become withdrawal instead of liberation.

Then, one morning in February, I woke in alarm to find the space in bed beside me empty. He had only begun to do this recently; to rise without waking me. I always hated that. In the early years he wakened me with kisses, or we woke together. But on this morning when I woke from the dream, I was alone. In the dream I had been talking to a woman who stood at the entrance to one of the houses in the road, indicating that she lived there. I told her all my inner thoughts for the sort of house I needed to return to. Suddenly I found that the woman, in listening to me, was growing more like me, the more I talked to her. She had taken my colours. We didn't actually change places. What happened was that the more I talked the less of me I became, the more of me she became. I did not become her in return, on the contrary I became no one. It was as though I was giving my identity away. It was from this dream that I awoke in mental fright to find him gone.

Disturbed, I got out of bed and looked into the mirror, where I noticed for the first time that I had become very fat. My face was swollen almost unrecognizably. Because of my size I could no longer wear the coloured clothes I had been wearing at Christmas. I fished from the wardrobe a large black dress which I had used as an overall for artwork at school. I fitted it easily. On reflection, I realized that Alice had begun to dress in the way I had previously. It was not the first time in my life that a dream had drawn my attention to something I consistently refused to acknowledge the existence of in waking life. In the old Hebrew stories or myths of ancient Greece and Ireland, people interpret dreams and act on them – or don't and are proved wrong. I am always too over-whelmed by the meaning of my dreams ever to do anything about them. The only course of action seemed to be to tremble uneasily and wait for disaster to strike. And it did. That evening I waited for their return. I knew that if the dream meant anything, something would happen soon. Paul came home alone and said: 'Alice isn't coming back; she has found somewhere else to live.' I sat down and cried with relief. 'Oh, I'm so glad, my love. I'm so glad. You have no idea what a struggle it's been for me, her being here.' But I looked at his face and saw that his eyes did not mirror my relief. Then he said, 'You don't understand. There's some-thing else I should tell you.'

There was a high-pitched whistle and then the sound went. I felt myself drifting away from his words. His lips moved but nothing came out. Afterwards, still in silence, I watched him leave the house. It's been silent for a long time now. I like it this way. It only gets noisy in here when Alice comes and that isn't often. But it's growing dark now and the nurses will soon come to put on the lights. I can't sleep in the dark in the silence. It frightens me, so they leave the light on. I still take photographs these days, but of houses, not of people: they're quieter.

SAM

What bothered me most about Sam, in those last few days before I left him, was his total exposure. All his emotions seemed to be on the surface. He would suddenly stop in the middle of the street, pull me towards him and put his hands up my skirt. Or he would lean across the table in the restaurant at lunch time, grab me by the collar and plunge his tongue down my throat. I got most of his lunch that way as well.

'Do you want the rest of this cherry?' I asked, extracting the stone from my mouth.

'Tinker, tailor, soldier, sailor, rich man, ' he said, counting five stones on his pudding plate. 'No, you keep it. I don't fancy being poor.'

I found this behaviour faintly baffling; I had been used to more reserve from my lovers in public places. (I said public.)

The following day he came to meet me in the street outside the china shop opposite the City Hall.

'Sam, you're out of control.'

'What?' he said, beaming innocently.

'Your fly is undone.'

'So it is,' he said, hitching himself up. His hands went immediately to my bum. He pulled me towards him and groaned: 'Oh, you feel so good.' I wriggled free, as the soldiers at a nearby checkpoint looked on.

I had come back to Belfast to kill myself, failing that I decided the next best thing was to love Sam. I told Sam I loved him. I told myself that I loved Sam; the problem was I didn't. Like most adolescents of twenty-seven and a half, I thought if you insisted something was true often enough it would begin to happen. I was indulging in childish beliefs again. I was also very bored. Nothing had ever lived up to the promise of my university days. I married another student who also read English. He turned himself into a successful journalist. We moved from Scotland, where we'd both been to university, to London, where he took a job with one of the better Sunday papers and that's when our troubles began. I had loved Scotland and hated England. I was terribly lonely and he soon got bored with me. Or was it the other way round: I was terribly lonely and I soon got bored with him?

We didn't have any children because he said he wanted to establish his career first. I should have taken the hint then. But I have always been a bit slow to see how I irritated people. A whole whispering campaign could be going on around my head and I would not notice. It took the girl from the next-floor apartment, a feminist who ran a battered-wives hostel in Islington, to say: 'He's left you, hasn't he?' I looked aghast and said:'Don't be ridiculous. he's only gone to work.' 'No. I mean he's lost interest.'

His first complaint was that I was too withdrawn; no one ever came to visit us. So I changed. Immediately I launched a series of parties; filled the flat with weekend guests; organized theatre tickets; joined a women's consciousness-raising group and took up yoga. Then he said I was too demanding and he wanted a quiet life. I began to feel confused. I went to see an analyst. A year later I left a note on the kitchen table, it read: 'I hope you find what you are looking for. I wish you all the best for the future.' Actually I think it was my lack of ambition which bothered him. All I ever wanted to do was read, bring up children and make jam. I should have written that note to myself.

When I returned to Belfast after eight years away, five of them married, I had no career and no job, however menial, to go to. I thought I might go back to university, because that was the last time I remembered being happy; except I had no idea what I would do when I got there. The day I got off the boat my father said:

'Well, I'm glad that's over. I never liked him anyway.'

My father was a widower living alone. I suddenly saw my

38

dilemma. My father was arthritic, my mother had worn herself away nursing him. He was glad I was back. But I was determined that two men weren't going to take advantage of my confusion. I told him I was getting a job.

'What do you need a job for? I've got money. You can live here for nothing. Sure I'd only have to pay a home-help.'

Mothering my father didn't appeal to me. In sheer panic at the prospect of what lay before me, I walked into an insurance office that afternoon at the bottom of Castle Street above the fish shop and took a job as a telephonist. I got on very well until the rest of the girls in the office discovered I had a degree – they stopped speaking to me. I was sitting outside the City Hall on a bench one lunch hour crying into my sandwiches when I met Sam.

'Oh dear. I'm sure it can't be as bad as all that,' a voice said. I had given up caring. I didn't even look up: 'It is. I've left my husband. I'm living with my father, and the girls in the office won't speak to me.' I completed this announcement with a great shuddering sob.

'Look, dry your eyes,' he said, taking a large, grubby hanky from his pocket. I accepted the hanky and his offer of a cup of tea just over the road. I discovered that he worked in a library and was writing a novel.

'What's your subject-matter?' I said. 'Or am I not allowed to ask?'

'War,' he said firmly.

I decided to ignore this. I invited him to come on a peace march with me. After the second peace march I decided to seduce him.

'I'll go to bed with you,' I said.

He was panic-stricken. I've never seen a man so frightened.

'Actually,' he said, 'I'm a virgin.'

'At least,' I said, retreating wildly, I wasn't sure if I could cope with the responsibility of it, 'I don't think we should go

39

on seeing each other if this relationship is to be purely platonic. It isn't fair on me emotionally.'

He agreed that it wasn't.

My analyst told me – I had an analyst in London after my marriage broke up – to have as much sex as possible, it would be good for me. It was with this in mind that I set out to seduce Sam. What I had not allowed for was the effect of as much sex as possible on Sam. We used to meet on Friday night after work and go to his house. We would go to bed immediately, make love, and then get up and have our evening meal – though not all of it; then back to bed, make love, get up and have our pudding; then back to bed again. In the morning, after lovemaking, we would cook and eat a hearty breakfast and then go back to bed before lunch. By teatime on Saturday, the bedroom had a very high aroma and I would be beginning to feel bloated.

I can't think why I didn't leave him earlier; I suppose I was rather fascinated by his gluttony. It was as though for the first time in his life someone had said to Sam: 'Eat as much as you like.' And Sam was so overwhelmed by the offer he ate compulsively and couldn't stop. My husband, the journalist, had been so terrified of vulgarity he never allowed me to eat apples or toast in bed. I never realized what a deprivation this was until I met Sam. We were two of a kind, we ate our heads off. And he had the most dramatic effect on my personality in other ways.

I dressed up every time I saw him. On some occasions I pretended I was Mae West and would slink along pouting when I knew he was looking my way. It was the best game I had played in years, I had a whole range of outfits that suddenly became clothes I wore when making love to Sam; a whole range of colours I could only associate with him. I seem to remember they were varying shades of fuchsia and lilac. My psychedelic suits were impressive enough even to win the admiration of the girls in the office, enough to minimize the handicap of having a degree. On the day I was to move in with him, I arrived in a shocking pink suit, green suede shoes and boa, reeking of Miss Dior. He opened the door to me, aglow with emotion, bent over to kiss me and banged his head on the lintel. It was classic Sam luck. It was also due to the fact that he was six foot three. Did I mention that before?

He was six foot three and he lived in the smallest house I have ever seen. 'Eh, why did you buy it, Sam?' I asked during my Mae West phase. I had had my hair cut three times in three months. The latest blonde perm had left me uncertain as to whether he would prefer me as Mae West or Marilyn Monroe. I decided on Mae West for myself. She was what you might call a survivor.

'It was different – cottage, you know.' He kept his head bent while we stood in the kitchen. 'I may have to lower the floor a little,' he said.

'Lower the floor?' I said. 'Why not raise the roof?'

The floor in the kitchen was already a foot below the outside step. The kitchen had one skylight window and gave the impression of being underground. It had been a weaver's cottage, recently modernized; but cheaply done; modernization did not dispel my feeling of being buried alive once inside it. However, I suppressed my unease about the place: after all, I had wanted to get away from father.

'Raise the roof?' Sam said. 'I hadn't thought of that.'

The next day was Saturday, it rained heavily and the water from the roof poured into the drain outside the front door. The drain overflowed into the hall. I was in the kitchen at the time and heard the water gushing; unfortunately I went to investigate. I had to ring Sam at work.

'Eh, Sam, I hate to worry you but the kitchen's flooded.

41

Could you come home and help bail out the water?'

Two hours later, when I had almost finished bailing water from the kitchen bucket by bucket into the sink, and thinking this is the last straw, two ambulance men appeared with Sam on a stretcher. He had slipped on the steps outside the library in the rain, slipped a disc and broken his ankle. Sam's luck had struck again. I thought of abandoning him then and going back to father, but it seemed a bit mean walking out on him when he was down. I stayed on.

Yet it wasn't so much that Sam was a danger to himself. I could cope with that, but he could also innocently project a certain destructiveness like radar on to anyone or anything else within his range; consequently he was extremely dangerous to be with. For instance, he was very fond of tomato juice and used to drink it by the gallon at meal time. One evening while we were eating he knocked over his glass, the rim cracked as it hit the table top and tomato juice poured over on to my lap, leaving an indelible red stain on my blue cotton dress, worn for the first time that evening. And he was often drawn to the most fragile object in the room: like the time he attempted to remove a very small scratch from an old china plate which had belonged to my mother. The plate was rather beautiful, so I had it mounted on the wall. Despite protestations from me, Sam took a piece of steel wool to the scratch and then a knife. The result was not the removal of the scratch but a gash ten times the size across the face of the plate. 'My hand slipped,' he said.

Another day at the open-air fitness centre at the park, I was moving along some parallel bars, shifting along on the strength of my arms alone. Sam couldn't wait until I was finished before it was his turn, he jumped up after me on the bars and began to move rapidly along the same short space. He knocked me clean off the bars, a drop of six foot, on to the grass below. I wasn't expecting the jolt, as he had already declined to get on them in the first place. I fell awkwardly. I think he said something like:'Oops, sorry. That was me,' and continued to finish the length of the bars before he stopped. He got off looking very pleased with himself, and then said: 'What's wrong with you?' I was kneeling on the grass nursing a crumpled limb and said in a voice of subdued rage: 'Sam, I think you've broken my wrist.' So it should come as no surprise that on the following Sunday, during a spell of sunny weather when Sam suggested he might take a look on the roof and try to mend the broken guttering, I fled out of the house.

'Couldn't you pay someone to do the job properly?' I asked. He accused me of having no confidence in him. I decided if Sam was on the roof I'd prefer to be outside the house rather than in. I put on my bikini, took a rug and lay on the grass at the far end of the garden, well clear of the house. Half an hour later I was sitting in the casualty ward of the Royal Victoria with blood pouring from my head. Sam managed to knock the ladder clean away from the roof – it was a direct hit. I should have left then, but the extraordinary thing was that I was so fascinated by the escalating violence of our relationship that I was spellbound into staying. I had read Freud at university, so I knew there was no such thing as an accident. He was full of remorse this time and brought me roses, said he'd never forgive himself and that he had a problem with objects.

And then it happened. We had very little money, but one day Sam went out and bought himself a very expensive piece of kitchen equipment. I was faintly surprised, we had been living on beans and eggs for months in one form or another and only ate meat occasionally. I looked apprehensively at the heavy, shiny stainless-steel blade and said: 'Eh, Sam, what's the meat cleaver for?'

'Chopping the legs off crabs,' he said. 'There's a recipe in

43

the *Sunday Times* for fish soup.' (I wouldn't let him buy the other paper for personal reasons. I am capable of that.) 'I fancied making it some time. It recommended a cleaver for the crab, so I thought I'd better get one.'

My occult sign was a crab – the spell broke.

I finally resolved to leave.

He was smiling when I said at breakfast several days later: 'Eh, Sam, I don't think we'd better see each other again.'

'All right,' he said pleasantly, and trod on my toe.

He went off to work as usual. There were no scenes, he offered no resistance to my departure. This surprised me. I thought the least he could do was throw himself on the kitchen floor at my feet and plead with me not to leave. As I had no immediate alternative, I went back to father. Sam was still smiling when he knocked at my door the next day. I was furious. Not with Sam, but with father. I had only just moved back and already he was making incredible demands on me.

'Yes?' I roared as I opened the hall door to him.

He was standing there grinning at me. My toe reacted in apprehension; I felt a slight stabbing in it. Had be brought the meat cleaver?

'Hello,' he said.

'Sam,' I said, changing into the alluring creature I always was with him. A few minutes earlier a vision of me in the kitchen rowing with father would have shattered that image completely. No, he would have to find someone else to water the cabbages and take the dog for a walk. Yes, I was only staying until I found a place of my own. Of course I couldn't commit myself to my whereabouts the day after tomorrow, I had yelled at my father. Standing at the door with Sam grinning manically at me, his hands behind his back, I wasn't sure if I'd be alive the day after tomorrow.

'I'm in the shit!' Sam said.

I concurred with this.

'I want you back,' he said. 'I'll do anything. I'll even lose weight.'

'Sam,' I said, trying to interrupt, but he continued.

'I'll be a great writer one day when my novel is published. I know I'll never do better than you and you'll never do better than me. We have to make the best of what we've got. Anyway, I'd like to have a family with you. So what do you say?'

It was father's voice behind me in the hall yelling – 'Who's that you're keeping standing at the door?' – which drove me over the threshold.

'Yes. All right, Sam, ' I said, playing for time. 'But come back tomorrow. I'm a bit busy with father.'

He was still smiling when I closed the door. He was still there in the morning when I went to bring in the milk. And he came back every night for a week and stood in the street until the fanlight in the hall went out. And he went away. He went away.

FIRST BITE

The wind woke me. The raging uncollected forces, that and the ringing of a cup. I was right in the middle of a dream about him. Disappointed, I got up. It had taken me weeks to get him back into my dreams again.

His face was white, chiselled, with a tear painted very carefully beneath his right eye. A chalk face, gaunt, with black eyes, and that mouth – not the wide mouth gaping, full-blooded elastic lips of the flabby-mouthed performers, his was finely shaped and crimson; a small mouth, full in the middle, and pinched at the corners, the bottom lip fuller than at the top, not spreading but holding firm at the centre. I imagined that kiss long before I took it. We lay; a wide canvas roof above, and broken straw like promises beneath us. The stable smelt of horse dung. I saw him in a ring of brightly coloured wood, performing with a spinning hoop of fire.

Of course, he wasn't a real clown, he was an actor; the straw was for effect, and the circus didn't exist. The horse dung was real enough, so were the horses. They belonged to the director's wife. The film crew moved out here from London to make a film about a circus. But I knew of him long before that film. I had seen him in a play he was touring with in Ireland once, and he stayed with me somewhere, a head and shoulders icon, so that when he looked along the table at me five years later, and fixed me with his look, I knew his face and smiled back.

Our coming to meet was like that, full of glances and significant stares. No words at all. Practically nothing was said, even in the stable all was silence. It was his face, the white, chiselled, lidless stare which drew me on.

Circuses have always excited me. The film was about a French circus and the clown was its star. They were filming

49

on the Cornish coast above St Just, because it was a low-budget production and the director, Jack, said that the Cornish coast reminded him of Brittany. 'It reminds me of Donegal,' I said. 'My goodness! Are you Irish?' said Margaret, Jack's wife. 'You don't have an Irish name.' They had taken a tin manager's house for the period of the film. It was a fourteen-bedroomed manse with enough room for the principals; the rest of the cast and technicians were housed in smaller cottages and farms round about. I arranged the accomodation and made myself so indispensable during the filming that I found myself staying on at the manse with them, which Margaret resented; she was particularly intent on keeping me away from him.

The second night at dinner he sat opposite and boldly out-stared me until I could neither concentrate on my food, nor the conversation on either side of me. She was sitting next to him, ever watchful.

'Have you been to many real circuses?' she asked me.

'Yes, at home.'

'Where is home?'

'North Antrim.'

I ignored her baffled incomprehension and rattled on before she could ask me where North Antrim was.

'There was a circus called Duffy's and I remember my first time vividly.'

'Really. How strange. I can remember my first visit to the theatre but not to the circus,' she said. 'What about you, Nicholas? What do you remember best, the theatre or the circus?'

'I was about five,' I went on heedlessly. 'And my mother booked the tickets weeks in advance. She never took chances on anything. Anyway, it was just as well because, the night before we were to go, the snake trainer was very badly bitten by a poisonous snake.' They were listening now. 'The local

50

paper carried a lurid description of the attack and announced that the trainer would nevertheless appear to do the same act again that night. So of course everyone in the town and for miles around turned up. It was just as well we had tickets. The trainer did appear and it was a woman. She had half her face in plaster and it was very inflamed where the snake had bitten her. Everyone waited for it to strike again. I remember she wore him round her neck like a fur stole; but he didn't bite again. I was terribly disappointed.'

'Charming,' Margaret said.

'I disagree,' said her husband. 'Apparently the snake didn't think so.'

'After the first bite, the poison goes,' I explained. 'So she wasn't in any danger.'

'Do you like snakes, then?' he asked, fixing me with his gleam.

'No, I prefer clowns,' I said, returning his look.

Margaret left us alone after that; until she and I were walking next morning with armfuls of hay towards the field where the horses were.

'That's quite a mane of hair you have,' she said.

'Thank you,' I said, tossing my head back.

'Nicholas is very interesting, isn't he? Don't you think?'

'Yes, I do.'

'He lives for his work, of course. Nothing else matters. That's why Jack loves to direct him.' We walked on a little further. 'He's a very good-looking man; women find it hard that he's so indifferent.'

'I've never found him indifferent,' I said, impishly.

She dropped the hay, having reached the appointed spot, and looked at me, lowering her lids until her eyes were almost closed.

'He has a wife and a child, you know. It's his second marriage.'

She raised her lids again, picked up the hay and walked to the far corner of the field with it.

After dinner, the cat walked from his lap to mine, and launched the full cup of coffee I was holding all over my dress. I put it in the washing-machine later and it shrank. The brownish-yellow stain is still there.

'I've got to change,' I said, getting up.

He was gone when I came back. So I went to the stable because I knew to. But he was nowhere to be seen. I was beginning to lose confidence in this game of no words and turned to go when a rustle of straw behind me drew my attention to his being there. I moved closer to the pale, immobile mask watching me from the corner of the stable; the white, gaunt face of a trickster, with a crimson smear.

'You said you preferred clowns,' he said, his eyes blazing, making the sockets moist until his mask ran.

A sharp hoof struck out against the tent wall.

All day I watched the wind pluck and tear at the leaves gathered at my door. 'You ought to brush them up. They won't do the concrete any good,' the woman from the flat above mine said, looking into the depth of the path. It was buried well beneath the steps to her front door. The leaves gathered stubbornly at my step and resisted all efforts of the wind to move them along. They had survived the autumn and hung over into winter – like myself.

'Let the wind move them,' I said. 'The wind brought them here. The wind can take them away again.'

She closed her door after that. She looked at me like everyone else did now.

Dead leaves cluster at my door and wallflowers I bought but hadn't planted in September (along with the rose trees and

52

tulip bulbs when I thought he would pass this way again) remained in the orange plastic bucket by the garden door. I looked recently and found their roots rotted from being too long in water. January, and still the rose trees stood in the torn packet in the kitchen, drying out against the radiator. Tulip bulbs lay unplanted, unprotected, blown by the November, December and now January winds from the safety of the sill to the slug-ridden stone path when he didn't pass this way again.

Well, at least today I got up. And the paper lad remembered me this morning, even if the postman did not. A bullying letter from a rejected lover a few days ago marked the New Year post; and a cheque yesterday from a patron – my ex to cover his misplaced guilt at going skiing at Christmas to the Swiss Alps with a friend. The first sign that he'd forgiven me. Guilt misplaced at going skiing at Christmas and leaving me here, broke. Hanging on too long, like the leaves at the door, I found myself on concrete instead of grass. And not enriching, not doing anyone any good. If only I had gathered up those leaves in time and spread them on the soil for the roses. I knew to. She told me several times, the lady upstairs. Tomorrow, I thought when I was moved to, every day as autumn drew to a close. I'll gather them up tomorrow.

The phone rang. I jumped. Could it be? He rang six weeks ago. They were filming near here, but only for a few days. 'I was very close to you last month. I nearly called in on you. But it was raining.'

A sharp kick against the tent wall startled me. Nothing. I said nothing. Radiating calm, cool, unconcern. I had wished for, concentrated on, that call. I had willed him to ring me. I'd also written and sent him some poems which told him nothing. He'd written back and said he loved them. Now he hesitated at the end of the line and I said: 'Goodbye,

53

Nicholas.' Inwardly I told him: 'I need more than this'; and put the phone down before he wanted me to, and knew I had. Afterwards for days, weeks, six weeks, I willed him to think of me. I concentrated too on dreaming of him. And twice now I have. The last time was today before the wind woke me and the ringing of a cup.

The phone rang on shrilly in another room.
  'Hello, Judith speaking.'
  'Did you get my letter?'
  'Yes. I preferred to ignore it. I hoped you would come to your senses.'
  'But I don't understand why. I don't understand.'
  Don't speak. Let him talk. He rang.
  'Can we meet?'
  'No. Please don't intrude like this. It's over, that's all.'
  'But you owe me a reason.'
  'Owe you? Why? We finished six months ago. Will you please stop writing to me. It's costing me a fortune sending things back.'
  'But why? I need to understand why you left me. I need to understand why it didn't work.'
  I fell back on the old euphemism:
  'I don't love you any more.'
  'Have you written much poetry recently?' he asked.
  'Practically nothing for weeks,' I said, glad to change the subject.
  (Six weeks could it be? And still no word.)
  'There!' he said jubilantly. 'You need me. To write.'
  Avoid at all costs telling him how much you hate him. Avoid telling him about the debts you incurred because of him. 'If you can't afford to go out with me sometimes,' he said once, 'just let me know, and we'll stay in.'
  'I don't see your car outside the flat these days. Have you

still got it?' So that's how he was brazen enough to ring. He's been watching.

'I sold it. Couldn't afford to run it. I was in debt.'

'You should go back to teaching. You could earn thirty pounds a day on supply.'

And a nervous breakdown every six months.

'Hello? Judith? Judith?'

I could still hear his dazed, baffled voice speaking into the dead line: 'But I don't understand why?'

Any more than I understand why I am waiting here after so much broken straw and the smell of horse dung; why I am waiting for a circus which doesn't exist and a man who is not really a clown; why I won't brush up those leaves from my door; why I am waiting for the wind to move, for the uncollected forces to take their raging course.

Why I wish; why I will dream of him again, his white, lean, chiselled face, through a bright ring of fire until the painted tear high up on his cheek's bone begins to melt, and drip, and run with the mask that once before ran, when we kissed, and smeared me crimson on the stable floor. After the first bite the poison goes, he reminded me. He said nothing original.

THE JOURNEY TO SOMEWHERE ELSE

The snowroad to the Alps runs south-east from Lyons to Chambéry, whereafter, leaving the autoroute behind, it takes up with a steep mountain road north to Mégève on the western slopes of Mont Blanc.

The resort café, several miles above the village, was full of seventeen-year-old French millionaires – or so it seemed to us – and large Italian families: the women wore fur hats with their ski-suits and too many rings for comfort; their men had paunches and smoked cigars at lunch; and the twelve-year-old Italian girls confirmed for all time that fourteen was the only age to marry and Capulet's daughter might never have been such a catch had she lived long enough to look like her mother. There were probably some large French families as well, but they were less inclined to sit together as a group. The resort on the borders with Switzerland and Italy was fairly cosmopolitan; confirming too that the rich, like their money, are not different but indifferent to frontiers. Whatever nation they came from, they had nannies for their children, who cut up the food at different tables and did not ski. On Christmas Day opposite me a black woman peeled a small orange and fed it to a fat white child, piece by piece. The smell did it: satsumas!

Christmas Day in '59; they ran the buses in Belfast; the pungent smell of orange brought it back. My brother, the satsumas in green and red silver paper on the piano in the parlour, the fire dying in the grate and the adults asleep in their rooms. And that year, in '59 when I was eight, it had begun to snow. The grate-iron to rest the kettle on squeaked as I pushed it towards the coals with my foot.

'You'll burn your slipper soles,' Michael John said.

'I'm bored.'

'We could go out.'

'How?'

'The bus passes to the City Hall every fifteen minutes.'

'They'll not allow us. I've no money and – '

'Ah go on, Amee. I dare you,' he said. 'Run out, catch the next bus to the City Hall and come back up on it without paying.'

'But the conductor will put me off!'

'That's the dare. See how far you can get. The person who gets furthest wins!'

My brother was small and fair and mischievous; there was ten months difference in our ages.

'All right then, I'll go.'

Joe is dark and tall and mostly silent; there is ten years between us.

'Would you like me to get one for you?' Joe said, putting the lunch tray on the table in front of me. 'Amee, would you like one?'

'What?'

'The oranges you keep staring at,' he said, handing me a glass of cold red wine.

'I'm sorry. No. I don't really like them very much.'

'You're shivering.'

'The wind's so cold.'

'Grumble. Grumble.'

'I'm sorry.'

With the life in the room the windows in the café clouded over.

'It would help if you stopped breathing,' he joked, as the window next to us misted.

It was a doomed journey from the start. Like all our holidays together it was full of incidents, mishaps and narrow escapes. Once, in Crete, I nearly drowned. I fell off his mother's boyfriend's boat and swallowed too much water. I remember coming up for air and watching him staring at me from the deck; he had been a lifesaver on a beach one summer, but I swam to those rocks myself. Four years ago in Switzerland, where he was working at the time, I fell on a glacier mountain, the Jungfrau, and slid headlong towards the edge with my skis behind me. I screamed for several minutes before I realized that if I continued to panic I would probably break my neck. I stopped screaming and thought about saving myself. At which point everything slowed down and I turned my body round on the snow, put my skis between me and the icy ridge and came to a halt. When I had enough energy I climbed back up. I suppose what happened this time was inevitable. About an hour after we crossed the Channel he crashed the car in Béthune. He drove at speed into the back of the one in front. I saw the crash coming and held my breath. On the passenger side we ended up minus a head-lamp and with a very crumpled wing.

'Why didn't you shout if you saw it coming?' he objected later.

'It seemed a waste of energy,' I said. 'I couldn't have prevented it happening.'

We exchanged it for a French car at Arrais and after I travelled apprehensively towards the Alps.

'Why don't we ski separately?' I suggested, after the first week. 'I'd like some ski lessons. Anyway, you're a far more advanced skier. I only hold you back.'

On the second day of that week I came back from ski class at four thirty and waited for him in the café by the main telecabin. There were so few people inside now the glass was almost clear. A family group sat at one table and ski instructors at the bar drank cognac. I waited for half an hour before I noticed the time.

It was snowing heavily outside then as well, and even getting dark. The snow was turning blue in the light. I closed the heavy front door behind me lightly till the snib caught and ran across the road to wait at the stop. I could see him watching at the lace curtains in the sitting room. The Christmas-tree lights were on in the room, the curtain shifted. Soundlessly, the bus arrived. I got on, and just as quietly it moved off. The conductor was not on the platform, nor was he on the lower deck, so I went to the front and crouched low on the seat and hoped he wouldn't notice me when he did appear. There was no one else aboard but two old ladies in hats with shopping baskets and empty Lucozade bottles. Noisily, the conductor came downstairs. He stood on the platform clinking small change; I could see his reflection in the glass window of the driver's seat. If I was lucky he would not bother me, I was too far away from the platform. Suddenly, he started to walk up the bus. I looked steadfastly out of the window. He rapped the glass pane to the driver and said something. The driver nodded. He spoke again. I was in such terror of a confrontation that I didn't hear anything he said. For a moment he glanced in my direction, and he remained where he stood. We were nearing the cinemas at the end of the road. At this point I decided not to go all the way round the route to the City Hall. I got up quickly and walked down the bus away from him and stood uneasily on the platform. At the traffic lights before the proper stop, he moved along the bus towards me, my nerve failed and I leaped off.

'Hey!' he called out. 'You can't get off here.'

It was snowing more heavily. Wet snow. My feet were cold. I looked down and saw that I was still wearing my slippers; red felt slippers with a pink fur trim. How strange I must have looked in a duffel coat and slippers in the snow. The clock of the Presbyterian Assembly Buildings read five forty-five. It chimed on the quarter-hour, and behind me the lights of a closed-up confectioner's illuminated a man I had not noticed before. 'You'll get your nice slippers wet,' he said.

'I'll dry them when I get home,' I said.

'You'll get chilblains that way.'

'No I won't.'

I looked doubtfully at my slippers; the red at the toes was darker than the rest and my feet felt very uncomfortable.

'Have you far to walk when you get off the bus?' he asked.

'No. I live just up the road. The bus passes my house,' I said.

'You'd better stand in here. It's drier,' he said.

I didn't answer. At that moment a young woman came round the corner into view and began walking towards us from the town centre. She walked with difficulty through the snow in high shoes. Under her coat a black dress and white apron showed as she moved. The woman looked at me and then at the man and stopped. She drew a packet of cigarettes from her apron pocket and lit one. At first she waited at the stop with me, and then, shivering, moved back into the protective shelter of the shop by the man's side.

'That wind 'ud go clean through you so it would,' she said.

'Aye. It comes in off the Lough and goes straight up the Black Mountain,' he said, looking away up the road. The woman and I followed his gaze.

Beyond us, a block or two away, was the dolls' hospital, we had been there a few weeks before with my mother.

'Leave the aeroplanes alone, Michael John,' she scolded. 'Just wait and see what Santa brings you.'

I loved that shop with all its dolls, repaired, redressed. My own doll had started out from there as a crinoline lady in white net with hoops and red velvet bows. That year, when we left it at the shop minus a leg, it had been returned to me as a Spanish dancer in a petticoat of multicoloured layers. We only ever visited the town with my mother; during the day when it was busy and friendly, when the matinées at the cinema were going in and the traffic moved round the centre, the cinema confectioner's shop in front of which I stood was always open and sold rainbow drops and white chocolate mice – the latter turned up in my stocking – so were there too, I noticed for the first time, satsumas in that window.

The snow, and the quiet and the darkness had transformed the town. In the blue-grey light the charm of the life went out of it, it seemed unfamiliar, dead. I wanted to go home to the fire in the parlour; I began to shiver convulsively, and then the bus came.

'Ardoyne.' The woman looked out. 'That's my bus.'

I was so grateful I forgot about the dare.

'No good to you?' she said to the man.

He shook his head and pulled up the collar of his coat.

'Merry Christmas,' she called out as we got on.

I was sitting brazenly at the seat next to the platform when the conductor turned to me for the fare.

'I forgot my purse,' I said. 'But this bus passes my house, my Mammy'll pay for it when I get home.'

'Oh, your Mammy'll pay it when you get home!' he mimicked. 'Did you hear that now!'

The young woman, who had gone a little further up the bus, turned round. We had only moved a couple of streets beyond the stop, the toyshop was behind me. A wire cage encased its shop front.

'Please don't put me off now,' I said, beginning to cry.

'I'll pay her fare,' the young woman said.

'Does your Mammy know you're out at all?' he asked and, getting no answer, moved along to the woman. 'Where are you going to anyway?' he called back.

'The stop before the hospital stop,' I said weakly.

'The Royal,' he said to the woman. The ticket machine rolled once.

'And Ardoyne. The terminus,' she said.

The ticket machine rolled once more and they grumbled between them about having to work on Christmas Day.

'I'll be late getting my dinner tonight. Our ones'll all have finished when I get in.'

'Aye, sure I know. I'm not off till eight,' he said. 'It's hardly been worth it. The one day in the year.' He snapped the tickets off the roll and gave her change. 'And no overtime.'

Someone, a man, clambered downstairs to the platform. He had a metal tin under his arm. The conductor pulled the bell.

'No overtime? You're kiddin',' she said.

'That's the Corporation for you,' he said.

Before the hospital stop he pulled the bell again. I stepped down to the platform. I could see the Christmas-tree lights in the bay window of the parlour. I jumped off and ran towards the house, and wished I hadn't been too ashamed to thank her. But her head was down and she wasn't looking after me.

Michael John opened the door: 'You did it?' he said, half in awe. 'I saw you get off the bus. You did it!'

'Yes,' I gasped. My heart was pounding and my feet hurt.

'All the way to the City Hall?'

'Of course.'

He followed me into the parlour.

'But look at your slippers, Amee, they're ruined. You went out in your slippers. They'll know.'

'Not if I dry them. No one will ever know.'

I put my slippers on the fender and stood looking at the red dye on the toes of my white tights. I pulled off the stockings as well and saw that even my toes were stained.

'Look at that, Michael John! My toes are dyed!' I said. 'Michael John?'

The front door closed so quietly it was hardly audible.

'Michael John! Don't go!'

From the sitting-room window I could see him crossing the road.

'Oh, I only pretended,' I breathed. 'I didn't.'

But he was too far away. And then the bus came.

I waited at that window until my breathing clouded the glass. I rubbed it away with my fist. Every now and then I checked the slippers drying at the fender. Gradually the dark red faded, the toes curled up and only a thin white line remained. I went back to the window and listened for the bus returning. Several buses did come by, but Michael John did not. I got under the velvet drapes and the lace and stood watching at the glass where the cold is trapped and waited. I could tell him the truth when he came back. The overhead lights of the sitting room blazed on and my mother's voice called:

'Ameldia! What are you doing there?'

She looked crossly round the room.

'You've let the fire go out! Where is Michael John?'

'Excusez-moi? Madame Fitzgerald?' the waitress in the café asked.

My ski pass lay on the table, she glanced at it briefly; the photograph and the name reassured her.

'Telephone!' she said, indicating that I should follow.

The ski instructors at the bar turned their heads to watch as I passed by to the phone. They were the only group left in the café. I expected to hear Joe's voice, instead a woman at the other end of the line spoke rapid French.

'Please. Could you speak English?' I asked.

She repeated her message.

'Your friend is here at the clinic in the village. We have X-rayed him. He will now return to your hotel. Can you please make your own way back.'

'Yes. But what is wrong?'

'I'm sorry?'

'What is wrong with him?'

'An accident. Not serious.'

'Thank you,' I said, and hurried away from the phone.

Outside it was dark and still snowing. I knew two routes back to the village: there was the mountain route we had skied down on after class a few days before, half an hour earlier by the light; and there was the route by road which

66

we had driven up on in the morning. I could also take the bus. It was five twenty. The lifts and telecabins closed nearly an hour before. The bus which met the end of ski class had long gone; so too had the skiers to the town. The only people left seemed to be resort staff and instructors, most of whom lived on the mountain. It took five minutes to ski down to the village on the mountain, and forty-five minutes to go by road – if a bus came. Without further hesitation I made the decision to take the shortest route back. It was too dark to ski, so I put my skis on my shoulder and started out to walk along the ski-track down the mountain.

I followed the path confidently at first, encouraged by the sight of three young men who were walking fairly swiftly ahead. Half-way down the hill through a farm, which even in deep snow smelt of farming, I passed a woman going in the opposite direction, who looked at me briefly and said:

'Bonsoir, madame.'

The surprise in her voice and the weight of the skis on my shoulder arrested me momentarily so I stopped: 'Bonsoir.'

I shifted my skis to my other shoulder and in so doing realized that I had lost sight of the other walkers ahead. I walked on to a turning point by a chalet and found there that the path forked two ways. There was no one ahead any more, and looking back uphill I found that the woman had disappeared. The lights of the village twinkled before me, directly below the treeline, luring me down the slope. The other path stretched more gradually down around the mountain. In the light it had been so easy. I stood for a moment staring at the mute grey wetness. Were there really two tracks? The longer I stood in the dark looking, the more confusing it became. If I don't move now it will be too late. I moved. I set off again rapidly downhill, but the weight of the skis on my shoulder and the slippery gradient propelled me onwards at a hair-raising speed towards the treeline. The hard plastic boots made it impossible to grip the snow. I

67

slipped badly and then stopped suddenly against the slope. My legs shook. I was breathless. If I moved another inch I would probably break a leg. Lost. I'm lost as well. If I could only be sure that this was the right way. Perhaps the wider, more gradual path is the one. I set off to climb back to the fork again. A light in the chalet further up the slope reassured me. I could always ask there.

Breathless, I regained the beginning of the two paths. I did not approach the chalet, but set out confidently on the wider path. The route ran between the snowdrifts higher on the mountain side than on the valley, but I saw also that now I was leaving the lights of the village behind, and this path, although easier to follow, was leading directly into a wood of pines above me. I came to a small grotto on the valley side of the slope, and beyond, a little further up the mountain, I could see the white stone façade of a closed church. A mound of snow nestling uneasily on the steep roof of the grotto slid off quietly in slow motion into my path, seconds before I reached it. Perversely, I plundered on. This is the wrong way, I'm sure it is, I thought. More precious energy sapped by the extra effort of wading through the drift, I came once more to a halt. The wind blew relentlessly. I noticed it for the first time. There is something noxious about the innocence of snow in its insidious transformation of familiar routes. I must go back. I turned and hurried back between the church and grotto, and reached, with a great deal of effort, the turning point on the path yet again. If I meet someone now, will they be friend of foe? If I go to that chalet to ask, will I be welcome? If I could somehow find the energy to climb further. I suddenly understood more perfectly than at any other moment that Fate, like a love affair, is a matter of timing: the right person passing at the right time; a combination of moments from experience which keep coming round like a memory, recurring, inducing in us the same confusion. It was as though I had stood all my life in the same cold place

68

between the curtain and the glass. How stupid I am. This whole journey is pointless, I said aloud to no one, I could have gone for the bus. I closed my eyes and breathed painfully.

'Where is Michael John, Ameldia? Why did you let him go? You're older, you should be more responsible! What bus? At what time?'

The conductor remembered him. He didn't have any money. No, he didn't put him off. On Christmas Day for thrupence? It wasn't worth it. He didn't remember when he got off. He hadn't seen him get off. There was a memorial service on the feast of the Purification; they waited and waited. There was no coffin, only flowers in the church, and my mother's tears all during the service. He went away so completely, he even went out of my dreams. Fair and small and mischievous.

When I opened my eyes a white mist was forming. I would have to hurry and get to the road before it enveloped me completely. Every step uphill was excruciatingly painful as again and again the skis bit into my shoulder. As I neared the top of the hill, passing through the farm smells, I heard voices. Two girls and a boy appeared, I went very slowly, passing them higher up the slope; I had climbed very high. They took the downward path, several feet of snow separated us. They did not glance in my direction and I had lost my curiosity about the route. We passed in silence. I got to the road again where I started out, exhausted. Did anyone pass him that night and not know?

Once on the highway I walked more easily where the traffic of the day had beaten down the snowtrack. My alarm had evaporated like the mist on the mountain. But I was hungry and tired and when I reached the car-park where the ski bus turned it was deserted, no one was waiting. I put the skis into a bank of snow and lay against them. My face burned, and my hair clung to my forehead from the effort and panic of climbing. A car passed. It was too dark to read my watch. If I walked on to the road towards the lights I would be able to read the time. I was too tired to move. My shoulders ached. I could not lift my arms above my head. My clothes clung. The backs of my knees were damp. My leather gloves looked swollen and bloated. Another car passed. It must be late; perhaps he will come out looking for me. If I go and stand on the road he might see me. I was too weary to move, so I stayed on. Then a familiar throaty rattle of an engine sounded, and a bus turned into the coach-park.

'Mégève?'

'Non. Sallandes.'

'Oh.' I must have looked disappointed.

'Dix minutes!' he assured me.

'Oh. Merci, monsieur!' I brightened.

He was back in half the time to pick me up. I dropped my skis into the cage at the back and in a few minutes we were hurtling down the mountain towards the village.

At seven thirty I got to the hotel. Joe was not there. The X-rays from the clinic were lying on the bed. Perhaps he was worried and has gone out looking for me, I thought. I was drying my wet clothes on the radiators when he came in.

'What on earth happened?' I asked at the sight of the sling.

'Oh, some idiot got out of control and jumped on my back this afternoon. Arrogant lout. He didn't even apologize. He said I shouldn't have stopped suddenly in front of him.'

'Why did you stop?'

'A girl in front of me fell down. I stopped to help her.'

'It's dangerous though, isn't it? You should have skied round her to safety and then stopped.'

'Well, anyway, I won't be able to ski again this holiday,' he said. 'The ligaments are torn.'

'Is it very painful?'

'It's a bit sore.'

'I'm sorry. Shall we go back tomorrow?'

'Well, we could go to Paris tomorrow instead of on Friday.'

'Let's do that, I'll drive,' I said.

'There's no need. I can manage. I have no trouble driving,' he said. 'How are you then, all right? Had a nice day?'

'Joe, I got lost on the mountain.'

'Did you?' he said. 'Oh, by the way, I've been downstairs talking to Madame. I told here that we were leaving earlier. She was very sympathetic when she saw the sling. She said she wouldn't charge us for the extra nights even though we've booked to stay till Friday.'

'I tried to walk down the path we skied on and then I couldn't find it.'

'That was silly,' he said. 'Why didn't you get the bus?'

'I don't know.'

It wasn't the first time in our ten-year relationship of living together and not living together that I found I had nothing to tell him. He never guessed the fury of my drama; and now he looked pale and tired.

'What's the matter?' he asked, catching me watching him.

'Nothing. Nothing's the matter.'

Even in Montmartre there was snow and coldness.

'There's a hotel! Stop now!' I said.

We had been driving all day, yet it seemed as though we never left the snowline.

'Stop! Please. That hotel looked nice. Joe, I'm not navigating a street further.'

'Ameldia, it's a five-star hotel!' he said, in a voice that reminded me of my mother. 'We are not staying in a five-star hotel!'

'It's on me,' I said extravagantly. 'Whatever this costs, it's on me!'

'But Amee, you don't have any money!'

'I'll argue with the bank manager about that, not with you,' I

71

said. 'I have a little plastic card here which will settle everything. Now, will you get out of the car? Please, Joe. You look exhausted!'

We signed into a fourth-floor side room. Through the nylon curtains I could see the traffic of Paris and the lights of the Eiffel Tower. 'We can walk to the Sacré Coeur from here. I think I remember the way,' I said.

My last visit had been as a schoolgirl fifteen years before.

There were tangerines in the restaurant – I lifted my head to them as they passed on the fruit tray to the table next to us – and ice-cubes on the grapes. I shivered involuntarily. I don't remember satsumas any other year.

'I forgot to ring my mother on Christmas Day!' I said suddenly.

'From the French Alps? Why would you want to do that?' he said.

'You know what they're like about me being away for Christmas.'

'No, I'm afraid I don't, I've never met them,' he said firmly. 'And I'm afraid I don't see why you think they should still be so obsessed with you. You are thirty years of age now, Ameldia, and you do have other brothers and sisters!'

'Yes, I know. But I was the only one around when –'

'Forget it!' he said. 'I didn't spend all this money and bring you all this way for you to drag that up now!'

'Madame? Monsieur?' A waiter stood eyeing us, his pencil poised like a dagger ready to attack his notepad.

Later as we passed through the square in Montmartre, sad-eyed artists were putting their easels away. An African spread out ivory bangles and elephants on a cloth on the pavement and I stopped to admire. He spoke English: 'Are you English?'

'No. Irlande.'

'Ah. Irlande is good,' he said, putting an arm around me and drawing me towards his wares. I felt like a schoolgirl again,

72

shy, drawing away, explaining I had no money to buy anything. Joe watched me from a distance and I said: 'Don't be
so grumpy.'

'I'm not grumpy,' he said crossly.

'Wouldn't it be nice to go and have a glass of wine in one of
those bars,' I said.

'Well, they look very crowded to me and I'm tired,' he said.

'Do you know why I love Montmartre?'

'No, but I'm sure you're going to tell me!' he said.

'Because whatever time you come here, it's always open, full
of people.'

I wished I hadn't brought him to Montmartre. He seemed so
uneasy amidst the haggle of trading in the streets. I had
forgotten how he hated markets. He did not relax until we got
back to the hotel.

I was not tired and didn't find that sleep came easily. My
tossing and turning kept him awake.

'Where did you get that cough from?' he asked.

'I must have got a cold somewhere.'

I got up and went to the fridge for a glass of mineral water,
and as I opened the door in the dark, I thought I smelt oranges.

'Did you spill the fruit juice?' I asked.

'No,' he said wearily. 'When will you go to sleep?'

I went to the shower room to drink the water so as not to
disturb him, and when I returned to the bedroom I found it
was very much colder than when I'd left it. The curtain
shifting slightly caught my attention. The glass in the window
was so clear it looked as if it wasn't there at all.

'Joe?' I called softly. 'Did you open the window?'

'No,' he said without stirring.

The room appeared to be filling with a white mist. It's like
on the mountain, I thought. The white mist of the night
outside seemed to grow in the room.

'That's funny.' The smell of oranges was very strong.
'Somebody is eating satsumas!' I said aloud.

73

Joe didn't answer. I got into bed and lay down trembling. The walls of the room were gradually slipping away to the mist. 'No. I will not watch,' I said firmly. 'I will not watch any more.' I closed my eyes tight against the dark and breathed softly.

Where the white rocks of the Antrim Plateau meet the mud banks of the Lough, three small boys netting crabs dislodged a large stone, when one of them reaching into the water after the escaping crab caught instead the cold hand of my brother. In May, a closed coffin filled the sitting room and the Children of Mary from the neighbourhood came to pray there and keep the vigil.

'I will not watch,' I said. 'I will not watch.'

An angel of Portland stone marked the grave and we sang: 'Blood of my Saviour wash me in thy tide'. 'He was bound for heaven,' my mother said often, and that seemed to console her. And every Sunday of the year we went to the cemetery, my mother and I; on Christmas Day ever after we left offerings of flowers and things until even the angelstone aged, became pockmarked and turned brown. It was the first Christmas I had not gone to that grave.

In the morning Joe drew back the curtains in the room and said: 'What a sight! I'm glad I didn't know that was there last night.'

'Didn't know what?' I said, moving to the window.

'Look!'

A huddle of stone crucifixes, headstones and vaults marked the graves which jostled for the space under our window against the side wall of the hotel.

'Montmartre cemetery!' he said.

There were no angels among the headstones.

'How creepy! Well, I'm glad we're going,' he said, with a last glance before dropping the curtain.

But I could still see.

'Last night,' I began to say, 'this room was very cold and I asked you if –'

'Oh, do come away from that window and hurry up and pack,' he said. 'We need to catch the lunch-time ferry.'

I wanted to tell him what I now knew, that the future was already a part of what I was becoming, and if I stopped this becoming there would be no future, only an endless repetition of moments from the past which I will be compelled to relive. 'It would help if you stopped breathing,' he had said. But it wouldn't; because there would always be the memory of existence – like a snare; a trapped moment, hungover in the wrong time. Unaccountable. And I wanted to tell him before it was too late that the difference is as fragile between the living and the dead as the absence of breath on a glass. But already he was rushing on a journey to somewhere else.

Bound for heaven, was it? Yes. Hand and foot.

LIFE LINES

The man in the next room whistling 'Stranger in Paradise' distracted me, again, for the twentieth time that day I put down my pen and sighed. It filled me with a strange and welcoming foreboding of – pleasure, was it? – an unexpected emotion in me. When I was young my father used to sing that. My father's singing haunted me down the years back to a time in a theatre dressing room when I sat among the greasepaint and the petticoats of the dancers. My mother made-up faces, and he sang in his vibrant tenor's voice: 'Take my hand, I'm a stranger in paradise, all lost in a wonderland'; and somebody called 'Shush!' from the top of the stairs, 'We're on in a minute.' Haunted me back down the years to a time when I was confident and sure I knew what love was.

And here I sat in another theatre, twenty years on, next to the dressing rooms, and stared out at the day, displaced, distracted, expectant; recalling the moment when he took me by the hand, walked me on to the middle of the stage and I stared up at the gantries of lights and breathed in. Oh, the ecstasy of it! I never doubted that the theatre was my home. I never missed an opening night when my father sang in those fifties musicals at a provincial theatre. Mother would want to send me home to bed or put me to sleep on the dressing-room couch, but when I pleaded my father would say: 'Oh, go on. She can sit in the wings with the prompt.'

I knew every song he sang; I knew his lines better than he did.

'Life isn't all a first night,' my mother used to say.

'I don't want her to be an actress.'

And he would wink knowingly at me, as if to say: 'And why not, kiddo? Why not?'

'Take my hand,' the whistle in the next room translated to a saxophone and then broke off. Minutes later it began – the musician walked into my room. He hesitated and then asked casually: 'We're going for a drink after work, will you join us?', adding the names of one or two friends; and equally casually, because I sometimes did on Fridays, I said, yes. He had done that before, come into my room and suggested a drink with the others. And when he had gone I closed my eyes and caught a glimpse of all those moments of his interest in me, hoarded by memory, like small stones of some beauty – what a miser I am – his touch on my shoulder in passing; the time he caught my hand under the table in a restaurant; or when he ruffled my hair in the car-park and whispered when no one was near: 'I like your hair'; and there too I saw in his silent watchfulness, in the dazzle of those small memories, hope in this dark corner, a hope I had allowed to grow, that I might still have the capacity to feel anything for anyone again. And I was blind and deaf to the chorus of 'Gabriel's so vain and flighty; Frances is so unhappy with him'; blind, but not so much, for in the coloured light of all those small reflections I saw something of my own image coming back at me, and it was not an honourable account by any means. I was still married to Jack, after all. If I felt that this was going to be different, it was only because I wanted him so much, and not even the presence of the woman he lived with, Frances, who was an actress with the company, could deflect my attention from him. If I had declined her friendship it was only because I was making way for this moment and I had guilt enough of my own about the past not to want to take on her accusations as well.

My father and I were friends until my first boyfriend came along, a policeman's son, who swept me off my feet, a tall Adonis – how I lived in myths! – who sent father off into a rage one Sunday afternoon because he caught us kissing behind the shed.

'You're too young for this! You've got your studies!'

Yes, and I still have; and sometimes when I put away my book or pen I wonder if we're not always too young for this emotion.

'Why don't you act?', he asked in the pub. 'I mean, with your looks.'

'Because I can't act.' I said, in my flat, northern Irish voice. The others departed to their women and homes, and late dinners, and smiled knowingly at us as they left. And someone cast a parting shot:

'Don't let Gabriel sweep you off your feet with his superlatives.'

Perhaps it was his lack of enthusiasm that attracted me.

'Have you eaten yet?' he asked.

When we were walking back to Jack's car at midnight I stood on tiptoe to kiss him – I was always standing on tiptoe.

He lifted me off my feet into the air:

'Yes?' he asked.

But you learn from experience, however late, that words drive feeling away, so I shook my head and kissed him again.

I was thirteen when I first stood on tiptoe to kiss that boy, the policeman's son; it wasn't my father's fury which drove him away, but my own chatter.

'My father was in prison, you know, before he was an actor,' I announced one day, proud of my uniqueness, as we walked hand in hand in the park.

'Really,' his grasp slackened. 'What for?'

'He was a political prisoner.'

'Oh, don't kid me,' he said shortly. 'You mean he was in the IRA.'

He let go of my hand while he searched for a cigarette. And I was so busy talking I didn't notice when he didn't pick it up again.

'I think you'd better go home now,' Gabriel said, and still held on to me, standing by Jack's car.

'Yes,' I said, afraid, and hurried away.

Doubtful of myself again; distrustful, in case some mischievous Puck – why is Fate such a malevolent spirit – or malignant Oberon had woken me at the wrong moment – again – in the forest – again – before the joiner with the ass's head. Gabriel was beautiful, but I didn't allow that to lull me. So, trembling, I drove home to Jack.

'Your eyes are very shiny tonight,' Jack said. 'I'm glad you're happy.'

And I made love to him instead.

And I didn't see Gabriel for a week after that, work intervened and kept me at home with new scripts we were planning for the autumn. Five days later, when I returned, he avoided me and I him. I could see him across the lawn with the other musicians and Frances at lunch, but I dared not cross over under all their eyes; my very tremulousness would give me away. All day I answered the dilatory questions of the office staff, directors and technicians about this and that, until, oh until, at coffee-time, suddenly looking up at the audio-library window, mid-sentence, I saw Gabriel there in the glass. Behind me and in front, he stood talking to the conductor. That day was surely the end of winter. The sun coming early in the year, welcome after the snows of the first few months, brought us out of our offices on to the lawn and he was standing reflected in the window. So suddenly had he appeared I never even saw him come.

'Teresa? You were saying? If we do the Greek thing, how much more time would the writer need?'

He was standing behind me, but I couldn't turn.

'Persephone is an interesting woman, don't you think?' someone was saying.

'I think the corn goddess theme could be better developed. Demeter's grief,' I said. 'But I don't know about the timing.'

82

And seeing in the library window that he was moving over to where I sat, I turned.

He stopped by me to put down his cup.

'Hello!' My voice sounded strange – what a formal greeting – and he smiled back. The sign that I needed. He moved away to the conductor and Frances once more. Once more I turned to face the sun, breathed in and closed my eyes, and began to hum: 'A stranger in paradise, all lost in a wonderland.'

Oh, why am I at the mercy of that man's smile! All day I'd fretted at my work, and yet it was enough to send me running for the shade and safety of my room. What a long winter it had been when it took only a smile from him and a soft kiss to set me breathing freely.

I don't think I have ever been so cautious in love, I had taken the initiative and acted on less in the past. With Simon, when I'd had enough of his innuendoes and his coy smiles, I simply said, when Jack was in the kitchen one night: 'Why don't we go to bed sometime?' But you pay for those moments at every turn and perhaps I didn't want all the responsibility of what happened next. So I said nothing to him that day, made no move at all in his direction. Alone again, I told myself that nothing would happen, but in my soul hope grew and grew until in Passion week, ten days after that first kiss, he came to my room again and said: 'Are you going for a drink after work?'

'I wasn't planning to, but I might.'

He hesitated.

'Here,' I said, giving him the number, 'ring me at home later. Jack's away designing a new hospital.'

At seven he rang, I got out of the bath to answer the phone, and at eight he came round.

'My father is an actor, did I tell you that before?'

He nodded: 'And you have to stop resenting him. You wouldn't have got very far without him.'

'Am I resentful?'

'We all are, we resent the best things in us. When I play, I think I'll never be that good again. And then I hate my music. I have to compete against my own talent all the time. You're a bit like that. You always seem to be at war.'

'The Irish are always at war.'

'That's no excuse.' He laughed. 'I've heard you arguing at the theatre. You're a terrifying person.'

'Do I terrify you?'

'No,' he said mildly. 'The saxophone is frightening some-times, too; it creates so big a sound, it takes you over. It's a very emotional instrument. I like that.'

We had planned to go out that evening, but he kissed me and we made love on the living-room floor. Love, was it? Some-how the word seemed inappropriate. It left me wondering how something I could have anticipated with so much pleasure could have caused me so much pain. I cried out – not the sound I made when making love with Jack in the woods – I like being out of doors – when I got mud on my shoes and the backs of my bare legs and leaves in my hair and inside I ran with him – Gabriel must have guessed because he looked at me strangely. What moment had he touched in me? Much later I lay in his arms, quieter, biting back the urge to say: 'Go away now, please, and leave me with this pain.' But instead I whispered: 'Will you stay with me till morning?'

All through the night he was telling me he was there in bed beside me. When I shied away he touched the small of my back until I returned, trusting again, and slipping his arm under my head we slept eventually. And those are moments of recovery. I remember how my father used to slip his arm under my head and snore loudly – when we fell asleep late morning after a show – while mother said: 'Keep an eye on her for me. I have to do the shopping.' Once I slipped so far below his arm he nearly smothered me with the covers. And I woke up wailing. That arm was a lifeline, it kept my head above the dark. And Gabriel beside me could never have known what he did. Now I know that adulthood is better than infancy; the short-temperedness of that time is what I remember. Joy spilling over into sorrow; smiles too quickly becoming tears; not all seas are calm, as not all days are, and these days I need a stronger line to keep me from drifting down.

It was Good Friday when we woke. The light was coming through the window blinds when we made love again. Opening my eyes, I saw for the first time what giving up this infancy of feeling meant – I wanted to cry out: 'Stop it! Stop it! You're breaking me!' I was raw, spent, and wondered if he was breaking, too. But I didn't trust him well enough to ask. Lying across me afterwards, he said: 'You're much too proud to learn anything from me.'
    The morning without mercy had caught up with us.
    'Jack will be here soon; we have to get up.'
    'What happens next?' he asked petulantly.
    The unspoken questions, about Jack? about Frances?, surface now.
    'I don't know,' I said; about what? Unable to find a qualifying phrase, I said nothing more, but my insecurity prompted me to ask: 'Will you ring me?'

After he had gone I went out into the day to buy some cigarettes – anything to deaden the impact – and walking back along the street I hurt so much and felt awash – remembering how young he looked; we were born in the same year, Jack and Frances were another generation. The traffic sounds seemed too harsh and the pavements too hard, and I found that even breathing made me ache and seemed too great a pressure. Until at eleven Jack arrived with some

85

primroses and an Easter egg in purple silver paper, for the one who usually slept with the light on because she was afraid of waking up and finding herself alone in the dark.

She is in love. Her eyes are shining and she has no energy. I've seen her like this before, many times. She's bitten down her nails and she hasn't combed her hair this morning. What a slovenly thing.

'You're smoking too much.'

'I know. I know, but who cares!'

Look at that ashtray! She must have chainsmoked through it last night. And wonders will never cease – she's done the washing up! If she's vacuumed the bedroom I'll know for sure. She's as jittery as a bird wandering around in her petticoat. Teresa in love! I could write a book about her. She'll start dressing up now and spending hours in front of the mirror, and not wearing any underwear. Then we'll have the poetry books out again; the love sonnets and Vivaldi at breakfast – or worse, those crackly old musicals she keeps playing over and over –

'Take my hand, I'm a stranger in paradise.'

Oh Lord, don't let her sing now!

'La, la, la, la, la, la, la – '

'What are your plans for today? Are you working?'

'I thought I might go to the Cathedral.'

'What?'

'The Passion. I thought I might go to the Good Friday service at the Cathedral.'

'I hope you're not turning religious on me. Is this an academic interest or what?'

'No, it's not academic. It's just something I'd like to do, that's all.'

'I thought you were an agnostic.'

'I never said that. I believe in — '

'What?'

'Forces.'

I wonder who it is? Somebody from the theatre, I shouldn't wonder. Who has she talked about recently?

'I've brought you an Easter egg. Aren't you going to open it?'

'No. I'll open it on Sunday.'

'Well, that's not like you. You usually can't wait!'

'These primroses are nice,' she said. 'You're very good to me.'

The Good Friday service at the Cathedral! That's the best excuse for having it away in the afternoon I've heard.

'Come here 'til I comb your hair.'

Why is it that husbands are so jealous of God? My father was just the same. He always made mother feel guilty. I remember when she took me with her to say the Stations on a Friday night, he would sulk at home or shout up the terrace after us: 'Tell her the truth! Tell her about the Pope's mistresses!'

Mother would say: 'Don't tell the nuns your daddy said that.' And Monica, my schoolfriend who was always with us, would giggle, because she came from a holy family – not theatre people – and her father would never say such things. Friday was confession night, when the chapel was full of incense and candlewax and the sighs of penitents; and although Monica and I weren't old enough for confession – my father said it was because our sins weren't interesting enough – well, I am making up for it – we used to sit outside the confession boxes, as close as possible, and try to over-hear the whispered sins of our neighbours – without much success. Once, when I got bored – once? – I was often bored – traipsing around the Stations after my mother, the purple-and-gold drape on the tabernacle caught my attention.

'What does IHS mean?'

'Quiet!' my mother said, kissing her crucifix.

'Maybe it's Christ's initials,' said Monica.

But I was always the doubtful one:

'Mammy, what does IHS mean?'

This time she was moving rapidly on to the final Station when she stopped and said, without hesitating: 'I Have Suffered.'

And looking up at Calvary we were overwhelmed by the simplicity of it; I remained so for many years, not even the sophistication of later knowledge shook my faith in that translation.

The Cathedral of St Peter and St Paul was not like the gothic parish church of my childhood. It stood, a grey stone wigwam, amid the Georgian streets; but then England is the frontier. Inside, it was as impersonal as an art gallery in its starkness; an affirmation, if any was needed, that the English Catholic Church has left the Renaissance behind. When my mother first came to this country to Mass in the Cathedral, she rushed out again thinking it was the wrong church. The Stations, she said, were shocking. And they were: strident concrete blocks with the eyes gouged out in grey cement; that single hand with the nail driven through the palm could have been a symbol of anything. Love and suffering. I sat on Good Friday in the afternoon as the crowd filled up the church, and ached, and thought of Gabriel. Why did he make me ache?

The priests came and prostrated themselves before the empty altar. Gone was the smell of incense, the candlewax and the whispered sins. Was it all so long ago? The responses were written on the paper I held, so I didn't have to think.

'He is not our King. Crucify him! Crucify him!'

I read my lines mildly. A procession passed through the church before me. There were two priests and two servers; the only purple drape in sight veiled the wooden cross they carried. The drape slipped nonchalantly off the wooden image as they processed down the aisle. He made me take off my petticoat, when that was all that remained between us. I didn't realize there was so much of me in hiding.

'Will you stay with me till morning?' Those were the hardest words I had to say.

'Lord I am not worthy, but only say the word and my soul shall be healed,' the words of the congregation seeped through. Only say the word. It was all that I came there for, but healed I was not. No miracle, just this casual ritual. And when they rose for the communion I left the church, still smarting, and wishing that I too could have the words written down somewhere, that I could say with all conviction and the confidence of my childhood faith, and envied the sureness of their response.

I walked back through the streets and thought the spring had never seemed so good and clear, and how things never really change: I was Jack's wife and would always be. On impulse I rang Gabriel from a call box, as if my action could cancel out the thought, and said: 'I'm missing you already!'

'You can't say that!' he objected.

He was right, but I wasn't deterred. Somewhere else I could hear my mother saying in the background: 'I don't want her to be an actress,' and see my father grinning: 'And why not?' Somehow it didn't seem to matter any more. A week passed before he rang me. There were narcissi on the lawn that day – a bad omen – but I would not be warned. At dinner he talked about Frances:

'She must never find out.'

Once more my rehearsed lines failed me, fled before me like Puck's grin. Was that mocking laughter in the restaurant an echo of his thoughts?

'She must never find out.'

Never. So that was it.

'Why are you seeing me?' I asked.

'Because every time I look at you I want to kiss your mouth.'

He did, across the table in the restaurant.

'Why don't we get the bill and go?' he said.

We made love again that night, and in the morning; before he went home to feed her cats and find her flowers waiting for him. (This detail is his confession.) I bled again, the absurdity of that endless taboo – 'does it make you feel virtuous to bleed,' he said, angry – and I felt my soul aching. Once, towards morning, I woke and caught his dark eyes – a deep, swift, glancing passion there, nothing still – before he turned his head away. Why don't you act? Because I can't.

In the late afternoon we went to an early film, and emerged still in the sunlight.

'I like going to the cinema in the afternoon,' he said, 'it feels slightly wicked.'

Oh, he was. We went to the pub where it had begun. He was such a conscious player, too clever for me by far.

'What time is it?' he asked.

I looked at my watch arm, and remembered he had criticized me for wearing my watch in bed, and had said mockingly: 'Aren't you going to ask me to stay until the morning?'

'Are you going to eat with me this evening?' I asked when I told him the time.

'No, I'm going to see a friend.'

'Ah.'

'What is your relationship with Jack?' he asked; it sounded like an afterthought.

'He's good to me. Though sometimes I think he'd be better off without me.'

'Frances would certainly be better off without me,' he grumbled.

'If there's anything wrong, it's probably my fault,' I added.

90

'Yes,' he said. 'That's my experience, too.'

I didn't tell him that I closed my eyes when I made love to Jack, or that he turned away from me in sleep. I didn't tell him that he had been my only hope; I never took my eyes off Gabriel. And there being so little that I could admit I lapsed into silence.

'Why are you so quiet?' he complained.

I only shook my head. Surprised as he was that the same force, as strong as the one which pulled us together, held my voice back now. He drove me home in Frances's car and parted with the words, 'See you,' and a kiss.

When I was a child we had a large mahogany Victorian sideboard, it belonged to my mother's family. Three feet off the floor it stood, with an overhead mirror as wide and long as the sideboard cupboard. It was the perfect stage. I often danced along it in front of the mirror, until one day, rehearsing the steps of the Christmas musical, I danced too far and fell clean off the edge, pulling the mirror and the contents of the cupboard down on top of me.

'She's broken all our wedding dishes!' my mother cried. 'This is your fault for encouraging her!'

But my father picked me clear of the debris, unscathed; so swiftly did he move I was tearless with surprise.

Tearless too, after Gabriel, alone indoors for the weekend as Jack was away – Jack was always away – I turned my face to another mirror and caught my old adversary staring back. Still the same – despite the deepening lines. I sat there so long my eyes, lips, the objects in the room, swam in the mirror before me, until, dizzy, I woke in time to put my hand out to stop me falling, and remembered in the flux of the room with all its swimming images, his glance in the morning, a dark swift passion – and no reflection in those eyes. I picked up the bedroom chair and drove it with the force that

91

kept me silent into the dressing-table mirror. It broke like a spider's web – bits of what was in the room still clinging to its lines.

And somewhere inside a still small voice woke up and called out: 'Mother!'

NAMING THE NAMES

Abyssinia, Alma, Bosnia, Balaclava, Belgrade, Bombay.

It was late summer – August, like the summer of the fire. He hadn't rung for three weeks.

I walked down the Falls towards the reconverted cinema: 'The largest second-hand bookshop in the world', the billboard read. Of course it wasn't. What we did have was a vast collection of historical manuscripts, myths and legends, political pamphlets, and we ran an exchange service for readers of crime, western and paperback romances. By far the most popular section for which Chrissie was responsible, since the local library had been petrol bombed.

It was late when I arrived, the dossers from St Vincent de Paul hostel had already gone in to check the morning papers. I passed them sitting on the steps every working day: Isabella wore black fishnet tights and a small hat with a half veil, and long black gloves even on the warmest day and eyed me from the feet up; Eileen, who was dumpy and smelt of meths and talcum powder, looked at everyone with the sad eyes of a cow. Tom was the thin wiry one, he would nod, and Harry, who was large and grey like his overcoat, and usually had a stubble, cleared his throat and spat before he spoke. Chrissie once told me when I started working there that both of the men were in love with Isabella and that was why Eileen always looked so sad. And usually too Mrs O'Hare from Spinner Street would still be cleaning the brass handles and finger plates and waiting like the others for the papers, so that she could read the horoscopes before they got to the racing pages. On this particular day, however, the brasses had been cleaned and the steps were empty. I tried to remember what it had been like as a cinema, but couldn't. I only remember a film I'd seen there once, in black and white: *A Town like Alice*.

Sharleen McCabe was unpacking the contents of a shopping bag on to the counter. Chrissie was there with a cigarette in one hand flicking the ash into the cap of her Yves St Laurent perfume spray and shaking her head.

She looked up as I passed: 'Miss Macken isn't in yet, so if you hurry you'll be all right.'

She was very tanned – because she took her holidays early – and her pink lipstick matched her dress. Sharleen was gazing at her in admiration.

'Well?'

'I want three murders for my granny.'

I left my coat in the office and hurried back to the counter as Miss Macken arrived. I had carefully avoided looking at the office phone, but I remember thinking: I wonder if he'll ring today?

Miss Macken swept past: 'Good morning, ladies.'

'Bang goes my chance of another fag before break,' Chrissie said.

'I thought she was seeing a customer this morning.'

Sharleen was standing at the desk reading the dust-covers of a pile of books, and rejecting each in turn:

'There's only one here she hasn't read.'

'How do you know?'

'Because her eyes is bad, I read them to her,' Sharleen said.

'Well, there's not much point in me looking if you're the only one who knows what she's read.'

'You said children weren't allowed in there!' she said, pointing to the auditorium.

'I've just given you permission,' Chrissie said.

Sharleen started off at a run.

'Popular fiction's on the stage,' Chrissie called after her. 'Children! When was that wee girl ever a child!'

'Finnula, the Irish section's like a holocaust! Would you like to do something about it. And would you please deal with these orders.'

'Yes, Miss Macken.'

'Christine, someone's just offered us a consignment of Mills and Boon. Would you check with the public library that they haven't been stolen.'

'Righto,' sighed Chrissie.

It could have been any other day.

Senior: Orangeism in Britain and Ireland; Sibbett: Orangeism in Ireland and Throughout the Empire. Ironic. That's what he was looking for the first time he came in. It started with an enquiry for two volumes of Sibbett. Being the Irish specialist, I knew every book in the section. I hadn't seen it. I looked at the name and address again to make sure. And then I asked him to call. I said I thought I knew where I could get it and invited him to come and see the rest of our collection. A few days later, a young man, tall, fair, with very fine dark eyes, as if they'd been underlined with a grey pencil, appeared. He wasn't what I expected. He said it was the first time he'd been on the Falls Road. I took him round the section and he bought a great many things from us. He was surprised that such a valuable collection of Irish historical manuscripts was housed in a run-down cinema and he said he was glad he'd called. He told me that he was a historian writing a thesis on Gladstone and the Home Rule Bills, and that he lived in Belfast in the summer but was at Oxford University. He also left with me an extensive booklist and I promised to try to get the other books he wanted. He gave me his phone number, so that I could ring him and tell him when something he was looking for came in. It was Sibbett he was most anxious about. An antiquarian bookseller I knew of sent me the book two weeks later, in July. So I rang him and arranged to meet him with it at a café in town near the City Hall.

He was overjoyed and couldn't thank me enough, he said. And so it started. He told me that his father was a judge and that he lived with another student at Oxford called Susan. I told him that I lived with my grandmother until she died. And I also told him about my boyfriend Jack. So there didn't seem to be any danger.

We met twice a week in the café after that day; he explained something of his thesis to me: that the Protestant opposition to Gladstone and Home Rule was a rational one because Protestant industry at the time – shipbuilding and linen – was dependent on British markets. He told me how his grandfather had been an Ulster Volunteer. I told him of my granny's stories of the Black and Tans, and of how she once met De Valera on a Dublin train while he was on the run disguised as an old woman. He laughed and said my grandmother had a great imagination. He was fascinated that I knew so much history; he said he'd never heard of Parnell until he went to Oxford. And he pronounced 'Parnell' with a silent 'n', so that it sounded strange.

By the end of the month, the café owner knew us by sight, and the time came on one particular evening he arrived before me, and was sitting surrounded by books and papers, when the owner remarked, as the bell inside the door rang:

'Ah. Here's your young lady now.'

We blushed alarmingly. But it articulated the possibility I had constantly been pushing to the back of my mind. And I knew I felt a sharp and secret thrill in that statement.

A few hours later, I stood on tiptoe to kiss him as I left for the bus – nothing odd about that. I often kissed him on the side of the face as I left. This time however I deliberately kissed his mouth, and somehow, the kiss went on and on; he didn't let me go. When I stepped back on my heels again I was reeling, and he had to catch me with his arm. I stood there staring at him on the pavement. I stammered 'goodbye' and walked off hurriedly towards the bus stop. He stood on the street looking after me – and I knew without turning round that he was smiling.

'Sharleen. *Murder in the Cathedral* is not exactly a murder story,' Chrissie was saying wearily.

'Well, why's it called that, then?'

'It's a play about –' Chrissie hesitated – 'martyrdom!'

'Oh.'

'This is just too, too grisly,' Chrissie said, examining the covers. 'Do they always have to be murders? Would you not like a nice love story?'

'She doesn't like love stories,' Sharleen said stubbornly. 'She only likes murders.'

At that moment Miss Macken reappeared: 'You two girls can go for tea now – what is that smell?'

'I can't smell anything,' Chrissie said.

'That's because you're wearing too much scent.' Miss Macken said. She was moving perfunctorily to the biography shelving, and it wasn't until I followed her that I became aware of a very strong smell of methylated spirits. Harry was tucked behind a newspaper drinking himself silly. He appeared to be quite alone.

'Outside! Outside immediately!' Miss Macken roared. 'Or I shall have you forcibly removed.'

He rose up before us like a wounded bear whose sleep we had disturbed, and stood shaking his fist at her, and cursing all of us, Isabella included, he ran out.

'What's wrong with him?'

'Rejection. Isabella ran off with Tom this morning, and didn't tell him where she was going. He's only drowning his sorrows.' Chrissie said. 'Apparently they had a big win yesterday. Eileen told him they'd run off to get married. But they've only gone to Bangor for the day.'

'How do you know this?'

'Eileen told Mrs O'Hare and she told me.'

'What kind of supervision is it when you two let that man drink in here with that child wandering around?' Miss Macken said, coming back from seeing Harry off the premises.

We both apologized and went up for tea.

There was little on the Falls Road that Mrs O'Hare didn't

know about. As she made her way up and down the road in the mornings on her way to work she would call in and out of the shops, the library, the hospital, until a whole range of people I had never met would enter my life in our tea room by eleven o'clock. I knew that Mr Quincey, a Protestant, from the library, had met his second wife while burying his first at the City Cemetery one Saturday morning. I knew that Mr Downey, the gatehousekeeper at the hospital, had problems with his eldest daughter and didn't like her husband, and I was equally sure that thanks to Mrs O'Hare every detail of Chrissie's emotional entanglements were known by every ambulance driver at the Royal. As a result, I was very careful to say as little as possible in front of her. She didn't actually like me. It was Chrissie she bought buns for at tea time.

'Oh here! You'll never guess what Mrs McGlinchy at the bakery told me – ' she was pouring tea into cups, but her eyes were on us. 'Wait till you hear – ' she looked down in time to see the tea pouring over the sides of the cup. She put the teapot down heavily on the table and continued: 'Quincey's being transferred to Ballymacarrett when the library's reopened.'

'Och, you don't say?'

'It's the new boss at Central – that Englishwoman. It's after the bomb.'

'But sure that was when everybody'd gone home.'

'I know but it's security, you know! She doesn't want any more staff crossing the peace line at night. Not after that young – but wait till you hear – he won't go!'

'Good for him.'

'He says he's been on the Falls for forty years and if they transfer him now they might as well throw the keys of the library into the Republican Press Centre and the keys of the Royal Victoria Hospital in after them.'

'He's quite right. It's ghettoization.'

'Yes, but it's inevitable,' I said.

100

'It's not inevitable, it's deliberate,' said Chrissie. 'It's exactly what the crowd want.'

'Who?'

'The Provos. They want a ghetto: the next thing they'll be issuing us with passes to come and go.'

'Security works both ways.'

'You're telling me.'

After that Chrissie left us to go down the yard to renew her suntan. Mrs O'Hare watched her from the window.

'She'd find the sun anywhere, that one.' She turned from the window. 'Don't take what she says too much to heart. She's Jewish, you know. She doesn't understand.'

I was glad when she went. She always felt a bit constrained with me. Because I didn't talk about my love life, as she called it, like Chrissie. But then I couldn't. I never really talked at all, to any of them.

The room overlooked the rooftops and back yards of West Belfast.

Gibson, Granville, Garnet, Grosvenor, Theodore, Cape, Kasmir.

Alone again, I found myself thinking about the last time I had seen Jack. It was a long time ago: he was sitting at the end of the table. When things are not going well my emotions start playing truant. I wasn't surprised when he said:

'I've got an invitation to go to the States for six months.'

I was buttering my toast at the time and didn't look up.

'I'm afraid I'm rather ambivalent about this relationship.'

I started battering the top of my eggshell with a spoon.

'Finn! Are you listening?'

I nodded and asked: 'When do you go?'

'Four weeks from now.'

I knew the American trip was coming up.

'Very well. I'll move out until you've gone.'

I finished breakfast and we spoke not another word until he dropped me at the steps of the bookshop.

101

'Finn, for God's sake! Get yourself a flat somewhere out of it! I don't imagine I'll be coming back.' He said: 'If you need any money, write to me.'

I slammed the car door. Jack was always extremely practical: if you killed someone he would inform the police, get you legal aid, make arrangements for moving the body, he'd even clear up the mess if there was any – but he would never, never ask you why you did it. I'd thrown milk all over him once, some of it went on the floors and walls, and then I ran out of the house. When I came back he'd changed his clothes and mopped up the floor. Another time I'd smashed all the dinner dishes against the kitchen wall and locked myself in the bathroom, when I came out he had swept up all the plates and asked me if I wanted a cup of tea. He was a very good journalist, I think, but somehow I never talked to him about anything important.

Because Mrs Cooper from Milan Street had been caught trying to walk out with sixteen stolen romances in a shopping bag and had thrown herself on the floor as if having a heart attack, saying: 'Oh holy Jay! Don't call the police. Oh holy Jay, my heart,' Chrissie forgot to tell me about the phone call until nearly twelve o'clock.

'Oh, a customer rang, he wanted to talk to you about a book he said he was after. Sibbett. That was it. You were still at tea.' She said, 'I told him we were open to nine tonight and that you'd be here all day.'

For three weeks he hadn't rung. I only had to pick up the phone and ring him as I'd done on other occasions. But this time I hoped he would contact me first.

'Is something wrong?' Chrissie said.

'I have to make a phone call.'

After that first kiss on the street, the next time we met I took him to the house, about ten minutes' walk from the park.

102

'When did you say your granny died?' he asked, looking with surprise around the room.

'Oh, ages ago. I'm not very good at dates.'

'Well, you don't appear to have changed much since. It's as if an old lady still lived here.'

He found the relics, the Sacred Heart pictures and the water font strange. 'You really ought to dust in here occasionally,' he said, laughing. 'What else do you do apart from work in the bookshop?'

'I read, watch television. Oh, and I see Jack,' I said quickly, so as not to alarm him.

'Good Lord. Would you look at that web; it looks like it's been there for donkeys!'

A large web attaching itself in the greater part to the geraniums in the window had spread across a pile of books and ended up clinging heavily to the lace curtains.

'Yes. I like spiders,' I said. 'My granny used to say that a spider's web was a good omen. It means we're safe from the soldiers!'

'It just means that you never open the curtains!' he said, laughing. Still wandering round the small room he asked: 'Who is that lady? Is she your grandmother?'

'No. That's the Countess Markievicz.'

'I suppose your granny met her on a train in disguise – as an old man.'

'No. But she did visit her in prison.'

He shook his head: 'The trouble with you – ' he began, then suddenly he had a very kind look in his eyes. 'You're improbable. No one would ever believe me.' He stopped, and began again. 'Sometimes I think – ' he tapped me on the nose – 'you live in a dream, Finn.'

And then he kissed me, and held me; he only complained that I was too quiet.

It was nine thirty when I left the building and shut it up for the night: Miss Macken had offered to drop me home as she was leaving, but I said I'd prefer to walk. There were no buses on the road after nine because a few nights before a group of youths had stoned a bus passing Divis flats, and the bus driver was hurt. The whole day was a torment to me after that phone call and I wanted to think and walk.

When I got to the park I was so giddy that I didn't care whether he came or not. My stomach was in a knot – and I realized it was because I hadn't eaten all day. The summer was nearly over – I only knew that soon this too would be over. I had kept my feelings under control so well – I was always very good at that, contained, very contained – so well, that I thought if he even touched me I'd tell him – Oh run! Run for your life from me! At least I didn't tell him that I loved him or anything like that. Was it something to be glad about? And suddenly there were footsteps running behind me. I always listened for footsteps. I'd walked all through those streets at night but I had never been afraid until that moment.

I suddenly started to run when a voice called out:

'Finn! Wait!' It was his voice.

I stopped dead, and turned.

We stood by the grass verge.

'Why didn't you ring me?' I asked, listlessly, my head down in case he saw my eyes.

'Because I didn't think it was fair to you.'

'Fair?'

'Because, well – '

'Well?'

'I'm in England and you're here. It's not very satisfactory.'

'I see.'

'Look, there's something I should tell you. It's – Susan's been staying with us for the past three weeks.'

'I see.'

I couldn't possibly object since we were both supposed to

have other lovers, there was no possibility of either of us complaining.

'But we could go to your place now if you like.'

I was weakening. He stooped to kiss me and the whole business began as it had started. He kissed me and I kissed him and it went on and on.

'I was just getting over you,' I said, standing up.

'I didn't know there was anything to get over. You're very good at saying nothing.'

And before I could stop myself I was saying: 'I think I've fallen in love with you.'

He dropped his head and hardly dared look at me – he looked so pained – and more than anything I regretted that statement.

'You never told me that before,' he said.

'I always felt constrained.'

He began very slowly: 'Look, there is something I have to say now. I'm getting married at the end of the summer.' And more quickly. 'But I can't give you up. I want to go on seeing you. Oh don't go! Please listen!'

It was very cold in the park. I had a piercing pain in my ear because of the wind. A tricolour hung at a jaunty angle from the top of the pensioner's bungalow, placed there by some lads. The army would take it down tomorrow in the morning. The swings, the trees and grass banks looked as thoroughly careworn as the surrounding streets.

Lincoln, Leeson, Marchioness and Mary, Slate, Sorella and Ward.

I used to name them in a skipping song.

The park had been my playplace as a child, I used to go there in the mornings and wait for someone to lead me across the road, to the first gate. Sometimes a passer-by would stop and take my hand, but most times the younger brother of the family who owned the bacon shop would cross with me.

'No road sense!' my grandmother used to say. 'None at all.'

In the afternoon he would come back for me. And I remember –

'Finn, are you listening? You mustn't stop talking to me, we could still be friends. I love being with you – Finn!'

I remember standing in the sawdust-filled shop waiting for him to finish his task – the smooth hiss of the slicing machine and the thin strips of bacon falling pat on the greaseproof paper.

I began to walk away.

'Finn. I do love you.' He said it for the first time.

I pulled up the collar of my coat and walked home without looking back.

It should have ended before I was so overcome with him I wept. And he said: 'What's wrong?' and took me and held me again.

It should have ended before he said: 'Your soul has just smiled in your eyes at me – I've never seen it there before.'

Before, it should have ended before. He was my last link with life and what a way to find him. I closed my eyes and tried to forget, all vision gone, only sound left: the night noises came.

The raucous laughter of late-night walkers; the huddle of tomcats on the backyard wall: someone somewhere is scraping a metal dustbin across a concrete yard; and far off in the distance a car screeches to a halt: a lone dog barks at an unseen presence, the night walkers pause in their walk past – the entry. Whose is the face at the empty window? – the shadows cast on the entry wall – the shape in the darkened doorway – the steps on the broken path – who pulled that curtain open quickly – and let it drop?

I woke with a start and the sound of brakes screeching in my ears – as if the screech had taken on a human voice and called my name in anguish: Finn! But when I listened, there was nothing. Only the sound of the night bells from St Paul's tolling in the distance.

I stayed awake until daybreak and with the light found some peace from dreams. At eight o'clock I went out. Every day of summer had been going on around me, seen and unseen, I had drifted through those days like one possessed.

Strange how quickly we are reassured by ordinariness: Isabella and Tom, Harry and Eileen, waiting on the steps. And Mrs O'Hare at the counter with her polishing cloth, and Miss Macken discussing her holiday plans with Chrissie. Externally, at least, it could have been the same as the day before, yesterday – the day before I left him in the park. But I saw it differently. I saw it in a haze, and it didn't seem to have anything to do with me.

'The body was discovered by bin-men early this morning,' Miss Macken said. 'He was dumped in an entry.'

'Oh, Finn, it's awful news,' said Chrissie, turning.

'It's the last straw as far as I am concerned,' Miss Macken said.

'Mr Downey said it's the one thing that turned him – he'll not be back to the Royal after this.'

'We knew him,' Chrissie said.

'Who?'

'That young man. The one who looked like a girl.'

'The police think he was coming from the Falls Road,' Miss Macken said.

'They said it was because he was a judge's son,' said Chrissie.

'The theory is', said Miss Macken, 'that he was lured there by a woman. I expect they'll be coming to talk to us.'

'Aye, they're all over the road this morning,' said Mrs O'Hare.

At lunch time they came.

'Miss McQuillen, I wonder?'

A noisy row between Isabella and Eileen distracted me – Eileen was insisting that Isabella owed her five pounds.

'Miss McQuillen, I wonder if you wouldn't mind answering a few questions?'

'How well did you know . . . ?'

'When did you last see him?'

'What time did you leave him?'

'What exactly did he say?'

'Have you any connection with . . . ?'

Osman, Serbia, Sultan, Raglan, Bosnia, Belgrade, Rumania, Sebastopol.

The names roll off my tongue like a litany.

'Has that something to do with Gladstone's foreign policy?' he used to laugh and ask.

'No. Those are the streets of West Belfast.'

Alma, Omar, Conway and Dunlewey, Dunville, Lady and McDonnell.

Pray for us. (I used to say, just to please my grandmother.) Now and at the hour.

At three o'clock in the afternoon of the previous day, a man I knew came into the bookshop. I put the book he was selling on the counter in front of me and began to check the pages. It was so still you could hear the pages turn: 'I think I can get him to the park,' I said.

Eileen had Isabella by the hair and she stopped. The policeman who was writing – stopped.

Miss Macken was at the counter with Chrissie, she was frowning – she looked over at me, and stopped. Chrissie suddenly turned and looked in my direction. No one spoke. We walked through the door on to the street.

Still no one spoke.

Mrs O'Hare was coming along the road from the bread shop, she raised her hand to wave and then stopped.

Harry had just tumbled out of the bookies followed by Tom. They were laughing. And they stopped.

We passed the block where the babyclothes shop had been, and at the other end the undertaker's: everything from birth to death on that road. Once. But gone now – just stumps where the buildings used to be – stumps like tombstones.

'Jesus. That was a thump in the stomach if ever I felt one,' one policeman said to the other.

Already they were talking as if I didn't exist.

There were four or five people in the interview room.

A policewoman stood against the wall. The muscles in my face twitched. I put up my hand to stop it.

'Why did you pick him?'

'I didn't pick him. He was chosen. It was his father they were after. He's a judge.'

'They?'

'I. I recognized the address when he wrote to me. Then he walked in.'

'Who are the others? What are their names?'

'Abyssinia, Alma, Balaclava, Balkan.'

'How did you become involved?'

'It goes back a long way.'

'Miss McQuillen. You have a captive audience!'

'On the fourteenth of August 1969 I was escorting an English journalist through the Falls: his name was Jack McHenry.'

'How did you meet him?'

'I am coming to that. I met him on the previous night, the thirteenth; there was a meeting outside Divis flats to protest about the police in the Bogside. The meeting took a petition to Springfield Road police station. But the police refused to open the door. Part of the crowd broke away and marched back down to Divis to Hastings Street police station and began throwing stones. There was trouble on the road all night because of roaming gangs. They stoned or petrol bombed a car with two fire chiefs in it and burned down a Protestant showroom at the bottom of Conway Street. I actually tried to stop it happening. He was there, at Balaclava Street, when it happened. He stopped me and asked if I'd show him around the Falls. He felt uneasy, being an Englishman, and he didn't know his way around without a map. I said I'd be happy to.

'Were you a member of an illegal organization?'

'What organization? There were half a dozen guns in the Falls in '69 and a lot of old men who couldn't even deliver the *United Irishman* on time. And the women's section had been disbanded during the previous year because there was nothing for them to do but run around after the men and make tea for the Ceilies. He asked me the same question that night, and I told him truthfully that I was not – then.

'On the evening of the fourteenth we walked up the Falls Road, it was early, we had been walking round all day, we were on our way back to his hotel – the Grand Central in Royal Avenue – he wanted to phone his editor and give an early report about events on the road. As we walked up the Falls from Divis towards Leeson Street, we passed a group of children in pyjamas going from Dover Street towards the flats. Further up the road at Conway Street a neighbour of ours was crossing the road to Balaclava Street with his children; he said he was taking them to Sultan Street Hall for the night. Everything seemed quiet. We walked on down Leeson Street and into town through the Grosvenor Road: the town centre was quiet too. He phoned his paper and then took me to dinner to a Chinese restaurant across the road from the hotel. I remember it because there was a false ceiling in the restaurant, like a sky with fake star constel-

110

lations. We sat in a velvet alcove and there were roses on the table. After dinner we went to his hotel and went to bed. At five o'clock in the morning the phone rang. I thought it was an alarm call he'd placed. He slammed down the phone and jumped up and shouted at me: "Get up quickly. All hell's broken loose in the Falls!"

'We walked quickly to the bottom of Castle Street and began to walk hurriedly up the road. At Divis Street I noticed that five or six shops around me had been destroyed by fire. At Divis flats a group of men stood, it was light by this time. When they heard that Jack was a journalist they began telling him about the firing. It had been going on all night, they said, and several people were dead, including a child in the flats. They took him to see the bullet holes in the walls. The child was in a cot at the time. And the walls were thin. I left him there at Divis and hurried up the road to Conway Street. There was a large crowd there as well, my own people. I looked up the street to the top. There was another crowd at the junction of Ashmore Street – this crowd was from the Shankill – they were setting fire to a bar at the corner and looting it. Then some of the men began running down the street and breaking windows of the houses in Conway Street. They used brush handles. At the same time as the bar was burning, a number of the houses at the top of the street also caught fire in Conway Street. The crowd were throwing petrol bombs in after they broke the windows. I began to run up towards the fire. Several of the crowd also started running with me.

'Then I noticed for the first time, because my attention had been fixed on the burning houses, that two turreted police vehicles were moving slowly down the street on either side. Somebody shouted: "The gun turrets are pointed towards us!" And everybody ran back. I didn't. I was left standing in the middle of the street, when a policeman, standing in a doorway, called to me: "Get back! Get out of here before you get hurt."

'The vehicles were moving slowly down Conway Street towards the Falls Road with the crowd behind them, burning houses as they went. I ran into the top of Balaclava Street at the bottom of Conway Street where our crowd were. A man started shouting at the top of his voice:"They're going to fire. They're going to fire on us!"

'And our crowd ran off down the street again.

'A woman called to me from an upstairs window:"Get out of the mouth of the street." Something like that.

'I shouted:"But the people! The people in the houses!"

'A man ran out and dragged me into a doorway. "They're empty!" he said. "They got out last night!" Then we both ran down to the bottom of Balaclava Street and turned the corner into Raglan Street. If he hadn't been holding me by the arm then that was the moment when I would have run back up towards the fires.'

'Why did you want to do that? Why did you want to run back into Conway Street?'

'My grandmother lived there – near the top. He took me to Sultan Street refugee centre. "She's looking for her granny," he told a girl with a St John Ambulance armband on. She was a form below me at school. My grandmother wasn't there. The girl told me not to worry because everyone had got out of Conway Street. But I didn't believe her. An ambulance from the Royal arrived to take some of the wounded to hospital. She put me in the ambulance as well. It was the only transport on the road other than police vehicles. "Go to the hospital and ask for her there," she said.

'It was eight o'clock in the morning when I found her sleeping in a quiet room at the Royal. The nurse said she was tired, suffering from shock and a few cuts from flying glass. I stayed with her most of the day. I don't remember that she spoke to me. And then about six I had a cup of tea and wandered on to the road up towards the park. Jack McHenry was there, writing it all down:"It's all over," he said. "The

Army are here." We both looked down the Falls, there were several mills that I could see burning: the Spinning Mill and the Great Northern, and the British Army were marching in formation down the Falls Road. After that I turned and walked along the Grosvenor Road into town and spent the night with him at his hotel. There was nowhere else for me to go.'

I was suddenly very tired; more tired than on the day I sat in her room watching her sleep; more tired than on the day Jack left; infinitely more tired than I'd ever been in my life. I waited for someone else to speak. The room was warm and heavy and full of smoke. They waited. So I went on.

'Up until I met Jack McHenry I'd been screwing around like there was no tomorrow. I only went with him because there was no one else left. He stayed in Belfast because it was news. I never went back to school again. I had six O-levels and nothing else.'

'Is that when you got involved?'

'No, not immediately. My first reaction was to get the hell out of it. It wasn't until the summer of '71 that I found myself on the Falls Road again. I got a job in the new second-hand bookshop where I now work. Or did. One day a man came in looking for something: "Don't I know you?" he said. He had been a neighbour of ours at one time. "I carried your granny out of Conway Street." He told me that at about eleven o'clock on the night of August fourteenth, there were two families trapped at the top of Conway Street. One of them, a family of eight, was escorted out of their house by a police-man and this man. Bottles and stones were thrown at them from a crowd at the top of the street. The policeman was cut on the head as he took the children out. The other family, a woman, with her two teenage daughters, refused to leave her house because of her furniture. Eventually they were forced to run down the back entry into David Street to escape. It was she who told him that Mrs McQuillen was still in the house.

He went back up the street on his own this time. Because the lights in our house were out he hadn't realized there was anyone there. He got scared at the size of the crowd ahead and was going to run back when he heard her call out: "Finn! Finn!" He carried her down Conway Street running all the way. He asked me how she was keeping these days. I told him that she had recently died. Her heart gave up. She always had a weak heart.

'A few weeks later Jack took me on holiday to Greece with him. I don't really think he wanted me to go with him, he took me out of guilt. I'd rather forced the situation on him. We were sitting at a harbour café one afternoon, he was very moody and I'd had a tantrum because I found out about his latest girlfriend. I got up and walked away from him along the harbour front. I remember passing a man reading a newspaper at another café table, a few hundred yards along the quay. I saw a headline that made me turn back.

'"The Army have introduced internment in Belfast," I said.

'We went home a few days later and I walked into a house in Andersonstown of a man I knew: "Is there anything for me to do?" I said. And that was how I became involved.'

'And the man's name?'

'You already know his name. He was arrested by the Army at the beginning of the summer. I was coming up the street by the park at the time, when he jumped out of an Army Saracen and ran towards me. A soldier called out to him to stop, but he ran on. He was shot in the back. He was a well-known member of the Provisional IRA on the run. I was on my way to see him. His father was the man who carried my grandmother out of Conway Street. He used to own a bacon shop.'

'Did Jack McHenry know of your involvement?'

'No. He didn't know what was happening to me. Eventually we drifted apart. He made me feel that in some way I had disappointed him.'

'What sort of operations were you involved in?'

'My first job was during internment. Someone would come into the shop, the paymaster, he gave me money to deliver once a week to the wives of the men interned. The women would then come into the shop to collect it. It meant that nobody called at their houses, which were being watched. These were the old Republicans. The real movement was re-forming in Andersonstown.'

'And the names? The names of the people involved?'

'There are no names. Only places.'

'Perhaps you'll tell us the names later.'

When they left me alone in the room I began to remember a dream I'd had towards the end of the time I was living with Jack. I slept very badly then, I never knew whether I was asleep or awake. One night it seemed to me that I was sitting up in bed with him. I was smoking, he was writing something, when an old woman whom I didn't recognize came towards me with her hands outstretched. I was horrified; I didn't know where she came from or how she got into our bedroom. I tried to make Jack see her but he couldn't. She just kept coming towards me. I had my back against the headboard of the bed and tried to fight her off. She grasped my hand and kept pulling me from the bed. She had very strong hands, like a man's, and she pulled and pulled and I struggled to release my hands. I called out for help of every sort, from God, from Jack. But she would not let me go and I could not get my hands free. The struggle between us was so furious that it woke Jack. I realized then that I was dreaming. He put his hands on me to steady me:'You're having a fit. You're having a fit!' he kept saying. I still had my eyes closed even though I knew I was awake. I asked him not to let me see him. Until it had passed. I began to be terribly afraid, and when I was sure it had passed, I had to ask him to take me to the toilet. He never asked any questions but did exactly what I asked.

He took me by the hand and led me to the bathroom, where he waited with me. After that he took me back to bed again. As we passed the mirror on the bedroom door I asked him not to let me see it. The room was full of mirrors, he went round covering them all up. Then he got into bed and took my hand again.

'Now please don't let me go,' I said. 'Whatever happens don't let go of my hand.'

'I promise you. I won't,' he said.

But I knew that he was frightened.

I closed my eyes and the old woman came towards me again. It was my grandmother; she was walking. I didn't recognize her the first time because – she had been in a wheelchair all her life.

She reached out and caught my hands again and the struggle between us began: she pulled and I held on. She pulled and I still held on.

'Come back!' Jack said. 'Wherever you are, come back!'

She pulled with great force.

'Let go of me!' I cried.

Jack let go of my hand.

The policewoman who had been standing silently against the wall all the time stepped forward quickly. When I woke I was lying on the floor. There were several people in the room, and a doctor.

'Are you sure you're fit to continue?'

'Yes.'

'What about the names?'

'My father and grandmother didn't speak for years: because he married my mother. I used to go and visit him. One night, as I was getting ready to go there, I must have been about seven or eight at the time, my grandmother said, "Get your father something for his birthday for me" – she handed me three shillings – "but you don't have to tell him it's from me. Get him something for his cough."

116

'At the end of Norfolk Street was a sweet shop. I bought a tin of barley sugar. The tin was tartan: red and blue and green and black. They wrapped it in a twist of brown paper. I gave it to my mother when I arrived. "It's for my Daddy for his birthday in the morning."

'"From whom?"

'"From me."

'"Can I look?"

'"Yes."

'She opened the paper: "Why it's beautiful," she said. I remember her excitement over it. "He'll be so pleased." She seemed very happy. I remember that. Because she was never very happy again. He died of consumption before his next birthday.'

'Why did you live with your grandmother?'

'Because our house was too small.'

'But the names? The names of the people in your organization?'

'Conway, Cupar, David, Percy, Dover and Divis. Mary, Merrion, Milan, McDonnell, Osman, Raglan, Ross, Rumania, Serbia, Slate, Sorella, Sulktan, Theodore, Varna and Ward Street.'

When I finished they had gone out of the room again. Only the policewoman remained. It is not the people but the streets I name.

The door opened again.

'There's someone to see you,' they said.

Jack stood before me.

'In God's name, Finn. How and why?'

He wasn't supposed to ask that question. He shook his head and sighed: 'I nearly married you.'

Let's just say it was historical.

'I ask myself over and over what kind of woman are you, and I have to remind myself that I knew you, or thought I knew you, and that I loved you once.'

117

Once, once upon a time.

'Anything is better than what you did, Finn. Anything! A bomb in a pub I could understand – not forgive, just understand – because of the arbitrariness of it. But – you caused the death of someone you had grown to know!'

I could not save him. I could only give him time.

'You should never have let me go!' I said, for the first time in ten years.

He looked puzzled: 'But you weren't happy with me. You didn't seem very happy.'

He stood watching for a minute and said: 'Where are you, Finn? Where are you?'

The door closed. An endless vista of solitude before me, of sleeping and waking alone in the dark – in the corner a spider was spinning a new web. I watched him move from angle to angle. An endless confinement before me and all too soon a slow gnawing hunger inside for something – I watched him weave the angles of his world in the space of the corner.

Once more they came back for the names, and I began: 'Abyssinia, Alma, Balaclava, Balkan, Belgrade, Bosnia', naming the names: empty and broken and beaten places. I know no others.

Gone and going all the time.

Redevelopment. Nothing more dramatic than that; the planners are our bombers now. There is no heart in the Falls these days.

'But the names? The names of the people who murdered him? The others?'

'I know no others.'

The gradual and deliberate processes weave their way in the

dark corners of all our rooms, and when the finger is pointed, the hand turned, the face at the end of the finger is my face, the hand at the end of the arm that points is my hand, and the only account I can give is this: that if I lived for ever I could not tell: I could only glimpse what fatal visions stir that web's dark pattern, I do not know their names. I only know for certain what my part was, that even on the eve, on such a day, I took him there.

FIVE NOTES AFTER A VISIT

Monday 9 January 1984

I begin to write.

The first note:

'You were born in Belfast?' The security man at the airport said.

'Yes.'

'What is the purpose of your visit there?'

To be with my lover. Well, I didn't say that.

I had written 'research' on the card he was holding in his hand. I remind him of this.

'I would like *you* to answer the questions,' he says.

'I am doing research.'

'Who is your employer?'

'Self.' I stick to my answers on the card.

'Oh! The idle rich,' he says.

'I live on a grant.'

I might have expected this. It happens every time I cross the water. But I will never get used to it.

'Who is paying for your ticket?'

'I am.'

'What a pity.' He smiles. 'And what have you been doing in England all this time?'

'Living.' Trying.

'There was a bomb in Oxford Street yesterday. Some of your countrymen.'

Two feet away some passengers with English accents are saying goodbye to their relatives. A small boy holding his mother's hand is smiling. Two feet between the British and the Irish in the airport lounge; I return the child's smile. Two feet and seven hundred years.

'He's a small man doing a small job!' Stewart says, when he meets me at the other side. 'Forget about him.' I won't. 'Now don't be cross with me. But you could save yourself a lot of trouble if you'd only write British under nationality.'

123

'I think – ' I start to say, but don't finish: next time I'll write 'don't know'.

I come back like a visitor. I always do. And I'm treated like one. On the Black Mountain road from the airport it is getting dark, when the taxi driver says:

'Do you see that orange glow down there? Just beyond the motorway?'

'Yes.'

'Those are the lights of the 'Kesh.'

Like a football stadium to the uninitiated.

'And just up there ahead of us,' he points to a crown of white lights on Divis ridge. 'That's the police observatory station. That's where they keep the computer.'

'Is it?'

'I had to do a run up there once. But I never got past the gates.'

We plunge down Hannastown Hill in the dark towards the lights of a large housing estate.

If I don't speak in this taxi, perhaps he'll think I'm English.

'What road is this?' Stewart asks, as we pass my parents' house. His father is a shipyard worker.

SINN FEIN IS THE POLITICAL WING OF
THE PROVISIONAL IRA

is painted on the gable.

WESTMINSTER IS THE POLITICAL WING OF
THE BRITISH ARMY

'This is Andersonstown,' the taxi driver says.

There is barbed wire on the flower beds in my father's garden. A foot patrol trampled his crocuses last spring. Tomorrow I'll go and tell them I've come home. But not yet. Stewart isn't keen.

124

'They won't approve of me,' he says. 'I've been married once before. They'll persuade you to go back to England.'

'They won't!' I insist. But I have the same old fear. His first wife lives in East Belfast.

Tuesday 10 January 1984

The second note:

I am looking at the bus that will take me to my mother. Through the gates I can see the others waiting too. I hear myself say: 'Mother, I've come back!'; and I hear her ask me, 'Why?'

I have let him lure me from my undug basement garden in an English town; one egg in the fridge and the dregs of milk; my solitude wrapped around me like a blanket for those six years until he came – and presented me with the only kind of miracle I ever really believed in.

I hear her ask me, 'Why?'

I remember the summer months, our breakfasts at lunch time in my garden, our evening meals on the raft, my bed. When term began again, he said: 'I've got a job in Belfast. Will you come and live with me?'

'Oh, I can't go back,' I said. 'I can't – live without you,' I tell him at the airport when I arrive.

I hear her ask me why?

My house is empty and the blinds are down. The letters slip into the hall unseen. The tanks will still turn on to the Whiteladies Road out of the Territorial Army Barracks and past the BBC. And the black cab driver will drive someone else from the station. 'Where to?' Blackboy Hill.

A For Sale notice stands in the uncut grass . . .

I hear her ask me why? I turn away from the stop.

Wednesday 1 February 1984

I have not kept an account of the days in between because I am too tired after work to write. And anyway I go to bed with him at night.

The third note:

It is the third day of the third week of my visit. I am working in the library.

'On the 1st of January 1957 the Bishop of Down and Conner's Relief Fund for Hungarian Refugees amounted to £19,375 0s 6d. Further contributions in a daily newspaper for that morning include: Sleamish Dancing Club, £5; Bon Secours Convent, Falls Road, £10; The John Boscoe Society for the Prevention of Communism, £25; A sinner, Anonymous —'

'Love?'

'£5. Three months later, in April of the same year, the Lord Mayor of Belfast welcomed the first 500 refugees. It was the only issue on which the people of Belfast East and West agreed.'

'Love.'

He is standing at my table.

'Oh, I'm sorry, I didn't see you.'

'Love. My wife's just rung. I'll have to go and see her. She was crying on the phone. She wants to discuss us getting back together. If only you knew how angry this makes me!'

'Will you tell her about me?'

Below the library window, voices reach me from the street. The students are assembling for a march. They shoulder a black coffin: RIP EDUCATION is chalked in on the side.

Maggie. Maggie. Maggie.

Out! Out! Out!

Police in bullet-proof jackets flank the thin demonstration through the square. The wind tosses the voices back and forth; I catch only an odd phrase here and there: 'Our comrades

126

in England . . . The trade union movement in this country . . '

'We have to keep a low profile for a while,' he said.

'And don't answer the phone in case it's her.'

When I was young I think, watching the demonstration pass, I must have been without fear. I make a resolution: I will go there after dark.

Thursday 2 February 1984

The Feast of the Purification. And James Joyce's birthday.

I always remember it.

This is the fourth note:

He is scraping barnacles off the mussels when I come back after midnight. 'Where were you?' he asks.

'I went to see my mother.'

'How was it?'

'She asked the usual questions. Did I still go to Mass? She said she'd pray for me.'

'Did you tell her about me?'

'I talked about my research: The Flight of the Hungarian Refugees to Belfast in '57. Can't think why. She said when I was leaving: keep your business to yourself. She was talking about you.'

'My wife cried when I told her. She thinks it's a phase I'm going through – and I'll get over it.'

There are pink and red carnations in a jug on the table, the man-next-door's music is coming through the walls. A trumpet. Beethoven. I'm getting good at that.

'He's obsessive,' Stewart says. 'He's played that piece since ten o'clock.' At the table I make a mistake: I push my soup away, I'm not as hungry as I thought.

'Go back! Go back to England, then! You said you *could* live with me!'

'I am trying.'

127

When I wake the smell of garlic reaches me from the bottom of the stairs. It was the mussel soup he lifted off the table. 'Go back! Go back to England! You're not anybody's prisoner!'

'I am trying!'

Mussel shells, garlic, onion, tomato paste, tomatoes and some wine, he threw into the kitchen. But the garlic hangs over everything this morning; and the phone is ringing in a room downstairs.

In some places, he said last night, amid the broken crockery, before a marriage they smash the dishes, they break the plates to frighten off the ghosts. Perhaps this is necessary after all.

When he wakes, I whisper: 'Love, I'll stay.'

'I've found you again,' he says.

The phone is still ringing in a room downstairs. It is 2.30 in the afternoon.

'Send your Fenian girlfriend back where she belongs, or we'll give her the works and then you!'

He is staring at the clock.

'I wonder how they knew?' he says.

'The estate agent has been writing to me from England. It was too much trouble to explain the difficulty of it. The postman would notice a Catholic name in this street. The sorters in the Post Office, too. Or maybe it was the man collecting for the football pools – '

'Football pools?'

'The other night a man came to the door, he asked me to pick four teams or eight, I can't remember now. Then he asked me to sign it.'

'You should have given my name.'

'I did. But I don't know anything about football. And I think I gave myself away when – '

'What?'

'I picked Liverpool! Or it could have happened at the

launderette when I left the washing in. They asked: "What name?" And I forgot. Or it could have been the taxi I got last night from here to – '

'I suppose they would have found out some time.'

He is sitting on the bed.

'Could it have been – your wife?'

He looks hurt: 'I never told her that!' he says. 'I suppose they would have found out some time. I think I'd better call the police.'

I get up quickly: 'Do you mind if I get dressed and bathe and make the bed before you do?'

'Why?'

'Because they'll come round and look at everything.'

I am packing a large suitcase in the attic where we sleep when he comes upstairs.

'The police say that anyone who really meant a threat wouldn't ring you up beforehand. They're not coming round.'

'Listen. I want you to take me to the airport. And I want you to pack a bag as well.'

'I'm teaching tomorrow,' he says. 'Please leave something behind, love. That black dress of yours. The one I like you in.'

It is still hanging in the wardrobe. I leave my scent in the bathroom and on his pillow.

'It's just so that I know you'll come back.'

At 3.40 we are ready to leave the house. The street is empty when we open the door. The curtains are drawn.

'We're a bit late,' he tells the driver. 'Can you get us to the airport in half an hour?'

In the car he kisses me and says: 'No one has ever held my hand so tightly before.'

'What will you do?' I ask, as I'm getting on the plane.

'I'll have to give three months' notice.'

'Do it.'

'Teaching jobs are hard to come by,' he says, looking around.

'Whatever this place is – it's my home.'

5.45. Heathrow. Without him I walk from the plane. Who are they watching now? Him or me? Suddenly, a man steps out in front of me. Oh, Jesus!

'Have you any means of identification? What is the purpose of your visit . . .?

Friday 3 February 1984

The fifth note:

A bell is ringing. I go cautiously to the door. I have slept with all the lights on. I see a man through the glass. He is wearing a combat jacket. This is England, I remind myself. The milkman is smiling at me.

'I saw your lights,' he says.

I tell him I've come back and will he please leave one pint every other day.

He tells me his son's in Northern Ireland in the Army.

'No jobs,' he shouts, walking down the path. 'Were you on holiday?'

'No. I was working.'

The bottles clink in the crate.

'It's well for some.'

He is angry, I begin to think, because I do not drive a milkfloat.

I am shopping again for one. At closing time I go out to the supermarket. It is just getting dark. There are two hundred people gathered in the road outside the shopping precinct. A busker is playing a love song. The police are turning away at the entrance the ones who haven't noticed.

'What is it?' I ask a young woman who is waiting at a stop.

'A bomb scare. It's the third one this week.'

I should think before I speak.

'There were fourteen people killed in London, in a bomb in a store.'

I am hoping she hasn't noticed. Some of your countrymen?

Then she says:

'Doesn't matter what nationality you are, dear, we all suffer the same.'

The busker is playing a love song. I am shopping again for one.

Noday. Nodate 1984

I keep myself awake all night so I am ready when they come.

THE WAY-PAVER

I rang my sister on the morning the baby was due and said: 'How are you feeling?'

'Bored.' She said.

I wondered then if I should tell her.

My sister has the habit of sadness. She was the second-born. The first-born child was me. My mother said the births were difficult – my third sister was left too long in the birth channel and suffered . . . they didn't have the equipment, they locked the forceps in a cupboard and couldn't find the key . . . was kept too long – that's when the brain damage occurred.

We were driving to the hospital, between the prison and the hospital, when I said: 'I must get some flowers.'

'Try Kennedy's at Carlisle Circus,' my mother said. 'We get all our wreaths from there.'

'I don't think that's quite the right place, is it?'

'It's still a florist.'

I tiptoed through the lily-wreaths and told the girl I was looking for a spray for my sister.

'She's just had a baby,' but I stood looking round.

'Why didn't you tell Maeve she was one of twins and the other was born dead?'

Eight months in the womb and the other dead. My sister is bitter about that sharing.

'It's none of her business. And it's certainly none of yours.'

My mother is secretive about her births – she has not prepared us.

'But you told Michael McMullen.'

'I told him when I thought they were going to get married.'

'She found out from him! Before he left her.'

'You're not suggesting – '

'No. I'm not.'

'Christine – that's a – stop!'

135

Red lights don't seem to signal stop.

'If you don't drive more carefully, I'm getting out to walk.'

At the hospital my sister was weeping. Her face flushed and hot. I pulled the curtains quickly round her bed, shutting out the other women in the ward – not their first time – who stared without emotion.

'I'm sorry we're late.'

'I thought no one was coming.'

'We stopped to get some flowers.'

'The baby's been awake all night. Every hour I've fed her.'

'Isn't that too much?' my mother said. 'Why don't you give her a bottle? I never breastfed any of you.'

I wish she wasn't so triumphant about it.

'It's all right, Maeve,' I told my sister. 'I was just the same.'

'Eamonn's mother was here. She doesn't like the baby's name. She thinks we should have called her after Eamonn's wee sister. She just kept saying: "My Mairead's come back."'

'I wish that woman wouldn't say those things. You can't call the living after the dead; your Granny always told me that.'

Eamonn's sister was killed when she was four. The dead child calls the living after it.

'You called the boys after Grandpa and Uncle Pat.'

They died in '46, and after that, in '47, my mother married my father.

'That's different. They weren't killed in an explosion.'

She still talks about that summer, at Malahide, away from the war; when Grandpa walked her up and down the shore collecting shells – his youngest and his favourite daughter. And Uncle Pat, her eldest brother, used to walk her home from dances. Many of them, her partners, she'd leave at the Scouts' Hall door: 'My brother's waiting.' He'd walk her home from dances.

'What did Uncle Pat die of ?' my sister asked.

'Tuberculosis.'

'And Grandpa?'

'A heart attack.'

'I never knew that.' More secrets. She puts on weight when she thinks about it. No one ever made it up to her.

'We went on holiday in August – there were German officers at that hotel . . .' My father never believed her. '. . . Ireland was neutral.' She insisted. 'They were both dead by Christmas.'

'Can I look at the baby?'

It was the sister from Waterford who got me through it.

'Use your pain,' she said.

'Push if you want this baby, you have to push it out away from you.'

That voice made me angry.

'You're four centimetres dilated,' they told me half an hour before.

'Let go! Let go of it!'

I remember the stillness of the room in between the calls to push – they thought I'd gone to sleep – but it was only my habit of breathing with my eyes closed.

'Ah, I don't think this is going to work,' I said when they tried to get me to breathe again.

'It's worked for thousands of years,' Sister Paul, a West Indian nurse, said.

My favourite brother is called Paul, so I grabbed her hand for comfort.

'Remember your breathing!'

'I can't do it! I can't do it!'

That's when they brought in the sister from Waterford.

'Now listen,' she said, using my Christian name, 'remember you are an Irish woman.' I hated her for that. The person I

137

hated most of all was mother – who was not even there. She had not prepared me. And Frank was helpless and beside himself. Earlier, Dr Hussain, the registrar, said: 'I think I should break your waters now.' I was alone in the room with them and the pains were coming so fast I said: 'Yes. Help me!'

That seemed the worst time of all, because I wasn't expecting it; afterwards when they went out I cried. Frank had gone to phone my mother – when he came back he didn't know anything had happened. I felt so betrayed; he promised he would be with me. I knew then that I was on my own. I thought of my ex-husband and Frank's wife – about whom I had never the slightest remorse: if I have committed any sins I am paying for them now. And God! Can this get any worse? The nurse from Waterford held my hand again and said: 'Now push! Use your pain.'

Another voice, a small nurse, English, I think, said: 'The baby's heart is tired.'
    The red pulse on the monitor dropped.
    'Her pelvis is so strong.'
    'I can see the head,' Dr Hussain said.
    'Push!'
    'I am pushing.'
    'Shush. Shush. There's no need to — '
    I was yelling.
    'Good girl, now use your pain.'
    Again.
    'Push harder.'
    'Will you let me cut you?'
    'The baby's heart is weakening.'
    'Push harder.'
    (They tried to stop me shouting, but I had to.)
    'Yes. Please.'
    Each time I pushed the head appeared; each time I stopped

the head withdrew. Immediately they swung my legs up into a strap, and placed Frank at the other end.

'Stand there now, and hold her hand.'

'The head's out!'

I cried out in shock. The head's free! And the long seal's back dived after it. Was there so much after the head? All that inside me? A genie uncorked from a bottle. The room was quiet, the baby quiet, only I was wailing. A woman's voice, I can't remember who, said: 'It's a boy.' I knew it would be. And Frank took up the chorus in awe and whispered in my ear: 'Oh love, it's a lovely little boy.'

Frank says, when it was first born, the child blinked, looked again, blinked, looked again, blinked and then stared. I remember only, they held him close to my face, he was folded in a blanket, like a letter peeping out of an envelope.

'He doesn't look very happy to see us!'

Worse. He didn't even look surprised.

And Sister Paul said: 'You've been here before, my lad.'

Once cutting, they pulled the head away from my body, with a stroke they held this head up with its long slippery tail. This seal, is my – son. These are the executioners.

'I don't remember any of that,' Maeve said at the hospital. 'When the doctor said: "It's a girl," I said: "How do you know?" And then I looked and he was holding her.'

'Everybody's different,' my mother said uneasily.

'I'm glad you told me it was going to be awful, though.'

'When did she tell you that?'

'When she phoned up. She said I'd feel like the survivor of a nuclear attack.'

'That's an awful thing to say!' My mother was livid. 'Why did you say that?'

'Because it's the most shocking thing that ever happened to me.'

Heart pain. Head pain. And after all these years – this: I went into hospital a proud, ambitious, talented professional, and I came out a snivelling schoolgirl, a crushed face in the mirror, a movable feast with leaking breasts, I felt suicidal at every suck. I didn't even like cats before. I was eight and a half stone when I found out I was pregnant; when I got past eleven I stopped counting. Angry? I am raging. It breaks out in gusts and I have to be restrained.

Yesterday, Oona and I took the baby for a walk. We could see the post van coming for miles. We pushed the pram into the hedgerow to let it pass; and caught up again at the next house along the road. He passed us and we passed him again and again during the walk, until, finally, we caught up with him when he stopped at the crossroads post box.

'Good morning.' We smiled.

'It's well for the women,' he said, getting back into his van and moving on to the next house.

Angry? I opened my mouth and shouted down the lane: 'Then let men have babies!'

Oona, the third-born, looked nervous, she's very wise in her way: 'Oh don't, Christine! Mr Delaney's a friend of my Daddy's.'

A nurse came and pulled the screens back.

'These flowers have just arrived for you. How's Maeve today?' She placed them on the bed. They were delicate, not brooding like the flowers I'd brought.

'She's nice,' Maeve told my mother. 'It's the night nurse I don't like.'

'They're from my sister,' my mother said, touching the corner of her glasses as she reads the card. Touching the corner of her pride.

'No cards from his side?'

'Mother!'

140

Nobody is good enough.

'I couldn't help noticing.'

She insists that she married down; my sister did as well. She scrutinizes my brother's friends, delights in Paul's promiscuity and in Pat's timidity. Oona, the third-born, moves heavily around my great-grandmother's mahogany with a duster and the noise of the TV in her head. 'Oona will always be with us,' mother says.

No one is good enough. I had to run away.

'Can you bring me a vase?' The nurse didn't hear.

'I must get water for these — '

'Mummy, leave them. The nurse will do it later.'

'The ward's too hot to leave them. I'll just go and get a vase from the kitchen.'

'Let her go. She likes hospitals. She knows what to do,' I said.

My sister and I have not been friends. The distance between us is too great to cross. Maeve once described it as not dislike exactly, more indifference. Only this confraternity of motherhood keeps us talking.

'How's England?' she says.

'I like it more and more.'

'Mammy says you have a lovely house.'

'We spent some time doing it up.'

'She seemed to enjoy herself that time she was over with you.'

'She was very good. I couldn't have managed without her.'

'Though she said the neighbourhood made her nervous.'

'We live in a red-light district.'

'Oh.'

'It was the only place we could afford to buy a house that size.'

'You know she lights a candle every night to St Martin' – hopeless cases? Or is that St Jude? – 'that you and Frank will get married.'

141

When the baby was ten days old, my mother answered the door.

'There's a lady in a sari and a boy. They want to come in,' she said.

'It's my neighbour.' Asha and Sultan; she has never called on me before. Asha looked into the cot and spoke in Urdu to her son.

'How big is it?' the boy translated.

'He's eight pounds,' I said.

'Would you like a drink?' my mother asked.

'A cup of tea or a glass of orange juice,' I explained.

'No thank you. I too fat. Too much sugar.'

'My mother has diabetes,' Sultan says,

'How many children have you?' my mother asked.

'Eight. How many you?'

'Five.'

I made friends with them when we arrived – Sultan and his sister Tswera were playing at the gate.

I said: 'Hello. I'm Christine and this is Frank.'

'Have you any children?' Tswera asked.

'I have a child in here,' I said, pointing. I was five months pregnant. They fled indoors laughing.

'For baby,' Asha said.

Sultan handed over a gift-wrapped parcel and a card. They had printed the names of all the children.

'Thank you. It's very kind.'

'She wouldn't have visited you, if you'd had a girl,' Maeve said when I told her.

Perhaps. At Ramadan, they sent us in a feast of chicken, rice, chapattis and pakhora. At Christmas we return the gifts. We don't know them any better than we did at the beginning. Asha makes my son laugh; when she sees him she always asks the same question: 'Baby all right? You all right?' She does not ask about Frank. And I have never seen her husband. Occasionally a ball comes over the fence or food is offered. We carefully wash and return all her dishes. She speaks in Urdu to her children. She comes from Northern Pakistan and she says abruptly 'Goodbye' at the end of a conversation. She goes along the hall and disappears indoors for another six months. She has eight births to consider and I have one. This is not her country, either. My mother picks up the gift she has left: a white woollen jacket and pants. 'It's expensive,' my mother says, surprised – the neighbourhood we live in is rather poor. The Council owns the house next door.

'When are you going back?' Maeve asks, as my mother comes along the ward with two vases of water.

'Not for another week.'

'Where's the baby?'

'Oona's looking after him.'

The third-born. The one and the locked door. My father kicking the door, the cupboard door, throwing the whole weight of his body against it, he told me – swearing, punching, the dull metallic cupboard banged like a drum against the wall. 'Open the fucking door!' Oona. That's when the brain damage occurred.

'Oona loves him. She watches all his little ways and tells us everything he does,' my mother says, arranging her sister's flowers.

'She's going to look after the baby when I go back to university. I didn't ask her to. She offered.'

'Yes, she told me.'

'You've got an au pair?'

Renate. 'Yes.'

At two and a half months I unhooked him from the nipple, gave him a bottle and handed him over to Renate. 'I have to work!' Occasionally I pass them in the hall or on the stairs – like two playmates, both new to this house; he's beaming, she talks to him in German – he's become 'mein Schatz' – while I watch and hope he'll remember something of me at the end of the day. And think of my own mother picking her way through her children's lives with her lighted candles and her prayers.

'Would you ever have another?' Maeve says.

'Another what?'

'Another baby.'

The prostitutes stand on the corners of the streets on the road to the maternity hospital, shivering in the sunlight in twos and threes. A few hundred yards away a group of Asian men are waiting outside the ante-natal clinic. They do not look at the prostitutes. They do not see them. The waiting room is full as Frank and I enter.

'No. 22 next!'

'Where's your co-operation card?'

'I'm post-natal.'

'Oh! You've had it,' the woman said. 'I still need a urine sample.'

I was peeing into the neck of a small bottle when she opened the hatch above me and called out: 'Are you Irish?'

'Yes.' I handed her the bottle.

'I'm from Tyrone myself.'

'I'm from County Down.'

'You had a difficult time?'

'Yes.'

'A boy, too?'

'Yes.'

'Well, the boys are always the worst. They've bigger heads than girls. Next time it will be easier. He stretched you, you see.'

'I'm not going to have another one.'

'Ah, go on. They all say that. You'll be back two years from now. It'll be much easier. The first one always paves the way.'

I went in to see the consultant and had a coil fitted.

The nurse came back: 'Excuse me – but you'll have to go now. Visiting's over.'

My mother looked around the ward to protest.

'Only fathers can stay,' the nurse said.

'Where is Eamonn?' my mother asked.

'He has an exam today,' Maeve said. 'Here – did I show you the photos? The baby ten minutes old. I bought Eamonn a camera for Christmas so he could take pictures of the birth, but we haven't got any – he fainted.'

When I looked up the three of us were laughing.

The woman next door weaves the names of her children on antimacassars in Urdu: my mother does not understand the country I have chosen.

'We thought you'd come home and have your baby here,' she says as we leave the hospital. I decided then that I should tell her.

'Mammy, Frank's just lost his job.'

'When?'

'Three weeks ago.'

'Why didn't you say so before?'

'Because I was hoping it wouldn't come to this.'

'But he seems so well set up,' my mother says. 'I don't understand this.'

'The grant to his department has been cut. He's the newest member of the staff so he's got to go.'

'Is his the only job that's been affected?'

'Yes. I think so.'

'You don't think he's been victimized because of us?'

'Because of us?'

'Your daddy's an ex-internee.'

'Mammy, that was in 1943.'

'Yes, but in '51 —'

145

In '51 . . . they came back.

'That time I went to visit you when the baby was born, and I didn't have any identification, I forgot the family allowance book and your daddy had to send it on.'

'I remember.'

'Well, I told the plainclothes policeman when I got off the boat that Frank was coming to meet me. And he asked who Frank was. All I could say was he's my – he's my – I couldn't find the right description and that made them suspicious. They weren't going to let me go until I said: "Frank's a professor of poetry." I think I even gave them his work address. Your daddy said I shouldn't have told them, they'd put Frank's name on the computer.'

'For what? Because he lives with an Irish woman!'

'But your daddy said – '

My father joined the IRA when he was fourteen, was interned at seventeen, released at twenty-one and met my mother at a swimming gala in 1947. He stopped seeing the republicans after that. They lived above a doctor's surgery in two rooms for a while and then Grandma took them back to live with her – when mother's elder sisters' opposition died down, or was too far away to matter. Aunt Eileen had gone to South Africa and Auntie Mamie to the London Civil Service. In 1951, when the King and Queen were visiting Belfast, they came back for him again.

'He's on night work,' my mother said – 'he's not involved.' I go back to that moment many times in my dreams, in the womb and on the stairs my mother stood, two hearts waiting, unable to move up or down to answer the pounding fists of the police on the door. Or was that sound her heartbeat and mine, in that safe dark place next to her breast? He was on night shift, so they went to his work looking for him. She did not see him for a week after that until the Royal Family were

146

safely back in London, and they released him. My father lost his job.

'I'm innocent,' he told his employers. 'My wife's expecting our first child.'

I was born then. I can hear that pounding yet.

'That was held against your father all his life. Only Catholics would employ him,' she says on the way back in the car.

'England is different,' I insist.

'Not at all. Everywhere's the same. Sure my sister Mamie was worried when I married your father that it would block her promotion in the London Civil Service.'

'And did it?'

'No. I don't think so. She did very well. But things have changed for us in England since the troubles.'

I knew she would say all this. Bring out the old stories, the old suspicions. That's why I wouldn't tell her.

'The new job didn't have tenure. The grant was cut. That's all. It's happening all over. There is no financial security any more.'

'What will you do?'

'Sell the house, send Renate back to Germany, go and live in a council house somewhere . . . how should I know!'

'Maybe something will turn up,' my mother says. 'It always does – and then you won't have to sell your lovely house.'

Habitat curtains and cork tiled floors.

'Mammy, Frank pays for everything. I have no money at all.'

'But you work!'

'Aye. The odd poetry programme on Radio 3 isn't going to pay the mortgage.'

'Well, I think it's time you gave up that writing and got yourself a proper job. You've a family to think about now, you've got to give your children some dignity.'

'I'm a poet. I don't want a proper job. Oh, I could work

147

as a shop assistant, but I had rather hoped to use all my intelligence.'

'You could teach somewhere. You've got an English degree.' I was waiting for this.

When my mother's eldest sister Mamie died in London, I was twelve, the money stopped coming to pay for Granny's big house. Aunt Eileen came back from South Africa to bury Mamie and bought her mother a two-bedroomed house in a quiet non-Catholic part of the city, two buses far for us to visit. We moved to a new housing estate on the lower slopes of the Black Mountain, Belfast West. Aunt Eileen gave us plenty of warning of her intention: she said for years we were too much trouble for her mother. My mother remembers it all. It was the first time we'd had to live on my father's income. The boys were born there, my mother had to give up her job, besides there was a rent to pay. For the first time we had to live on father's income and of course we didn't. My mother remembers it all. It was three miles to the nearest bus. It took five years before the city boundary was extended – before a red bus passed our front door. My mother didn't like the housing estate. My father promised he'd look around for something better. She wanted a nice house on the lough. My mother remembers it all. She pinned her hopes on her first-born finishing school and getting a proper job, so they could buy a house at the sea. I couldn't take the responsibility of it. After six years I ran away to university – England – and I never came back. Me. The first-born. The way-paver. The one who ran. I married a man who was careful with money, a teacher, with a house of his own. I was so desperate to marry that man. I wrote and told them I was getting married and could they lend me £200 to pay for the wedding. I kept him away from my family until it was too late. I was so desperate. And I was successful. They found the money. We were married in England: only my father and mother came.

148

They got off the plane at Heathrow on the day before the wedding and left by the following day's flight. I remember how they hurried away at the airport.

I never took him back to see the house, on the side of the Black Mountain, with the battered front door – my brothers kicked it when they wanted in – the brunt of so many small tantrums. Andersonstown, my mother lived there for eighteen years. I put the Irish sea between me and that memory. And I wanted so much to be a poet. Except once when Maeve was getting married, seven years after my own, we went back for the wedding. And he saw it all. The house, the battered door and torn garden. The estate graffiti, the flags and emblems of resistance. The wedding was massive. My mother saved her family allowance for years, for the peach two-piece she wore, the orchids, and the singer at the Mass; the 200 sit-down in a local hotel. I knew it was going to be like that. My husband said: 'Your father doesn't spend his money on the house, does he?' He'd expected so much more. I had not prepared him. When we went back to England, I gave up my job; I'd been threatening to for years. I want to be a poet, I said. I invited him to abandon me. Which is strange, when I was once so desperate to marry that man. Desperation runs in generations in my family.

I never wanted to marry Frank. He was my lover. I wanted to live with him sometimes and then I found I was pregnant and everything changed. Frank was a professor of literature and the editor of a poetry review. I walked into his office, when he'd read some poems I sent him, and he'd asked to see me. I walked into his office and I thought: No, I am not going to fall in love with this man. Frank's wife said, when he left her, I'd hardly made a disinterested choice of lover, a professor and the editor of a review. He published my poems. The accusation stuck. But I didn't care. He changed jobs when I was five months on, to get away from the gossip. We moved to another part of the country. And he gave up the review. I didn't expect or hope anything would last. We always seemed to be just minutes ahead of destruction before the baby was born. But I went on writing and then everything changed. When he came home late that Friday night three weeks ago and told me he'd lost his job, I knew when he got out of the car in the rain, two hours late for supper.

I once asked Asha where her husband was; she had a year-old child on her knee. He goes out, she told me, every morning early, he takes his bicycle and he comes back after dark. 'What work does he do?' I asked.

'No work,' she said. 'He no work.'

The journey from the hospital in Belfast takes about an hour along the coast. The road runs past the cottage a little on to pebble, then grass, then rock; below, the waves of the Irish Sea wash the ridge of the peninsula – the first vanguard of the land into the sea. On this unofficial headland the house stands.

'You can see Scotland on a clear day and just over there the Isle of Man,' the estate agent told my father three years ago when they retired to the cottage on the Point. He kept his promise. My sister Oona is waiting at the door with my son in her arms when we drive up. They are watching the gulls. He cries out when he sees me. His new voice catches me unawares.

'That's a strange sound.'

'He thinks he's a gull,' Oona said.

My mother looks depressed by this sudden insecurity. I didn't tell her about the tax assessments for more than the price of our house; or the appeal we won in the spring; or the burglary – not surprising in our neighbourhood . . . always minutes ahead of destruction . . . I didn't tell her . . . England is the country I have chosen for my son – and like Asha and Sultan, I need to believe in it.

Then I say: 'I'm thinking of getting married – when Frank's divorce comes through.'

She looks out across the water.

'I like Frank,' she says.

Fifteen years ago I put more than the Irish Sea between myself and my family.

Further up the estuary on the other side of the peninsula is a seal colony. Once in a while one or two swim out and make for the open sea; we watch for these from the rocks in front of the cottage.

'They look so human,' my mother says, as a head breaks the water, paving the way. We concentrate on that stray seal.